THE ZEPPELIN BEND

unraveling the knot of deception

THE ZEPPELIN BEND

unraveling the knot of deception

DONNALEE OVERLY

Giro di Mondo

For permission, please write to Giro di Mondo Publishing, a division of the Ottima Group, 1417 Sadler Rod, Suite 332, Amelia Island, FL 32034, or email info@girodimondo.com.
Printed in the United States of America.
First Edition, October, 2018
10 9 8 7 6 4 3 1 `

Cover and Interior design by Roseanna White Designs
Zeppelin Bend knot artwork by DonnaLee Overly

Library of Congress Control Number: 2018952954

ISBN Trade Paperback- 978-0-9966687-5-0
ISBN EBOOK - 978-0-9966687-6-7

Published by:
Giro di Mondo Publishing Services
Amelia Island, Florida
www.girodimondo.com

Dedicated to all women who had to make a difficult choice.

A ZEPPELIN BEND

is a knot formed with two separate ropes
and when under stress the knot becomes tighter.

"I find that I have painted my life-things happening in my life-without knowing."
1976, Georgia O'Keefe (1887-1986)

PART 1

CHAPTER 1

Gabby

G od, please let this be a mistake." As soon as the words escape her lips, Gabby's body starts trembling. Her fingers lose their grip on the white plastic strip, and it flutters to the bathroom floor. The plus sign stands out clearly against the beige-colored tile. Turning toward the mirror, the pale face that stares back looks foreign, and she can't control the whimper that leaves her throat. She sounds like a wounded animal. *Did I make that noise?*

With shaky legs, she lowers herself onto the white throne. She fights tears and chokes back her sobs. She inhales a deep breath and slowly lets it out. These past few weeks, life has been almost perfect. This was not in her plan.

Gabby pinches her lips tight and probes the deep corners of her brain. Tracing back the events of the past few months since she has been dating Brett, her tennis pro with a signature dimple, her life and her calendar have been gloriously full. First, Richard, her former boyfriend of two years, moved out of her condo. Then, she and Brett went to the ranch to help her dad with the cattle branding, and lastly, they helped with the preparations for her father's wedding. *Think, Gabby, think, when was your last period?*

"Pull yourself together," she scolds herself out loud as she stands to flush and clean up with shaky hands. Then she smoothes her hair and straightens her skirt. She can't hide in this bathroom forever. In just two short minutes, she has learned that her life must take a new direction. Turning the knob, she exits the tiny room and shuts the door gently, recognizing that she's leaving her dreams behind, and entering her new world.

One week earlier

Grateful for the quiet, Gabby gives a big sigh as she rocks back and forth in the chair on the double ranch house's wraparound porch. It feels good to sit and rest. The blue ribbons on the posts sag, and the flowers hang their heads. Everyone is weary from the day's activities. The corners of her mouth turn up slightly because she feels those inanimate objects share her thoughts.

Even though she is weary, it was a grand day. A day full of the promise of a bright future for the hopeful couple. Now, the day has ended. She feels the cool, gentle breeze on her face as evening settles in. Rocking back and forth and mesmerized by the rhythmic moans of the wooden porch, she brings to mind the details of the day as she watches the last of the car lights fade away into the distant Texas horizon.

Looking up to the heavens, she smiles at the stars gracing the evening with their presence. She lifts her wine glass and whispers, "Here's to you, Mother."

After giving a voice to these words, she blinks back a tear. Her hand automatically grasps her trinity knot necklace and she slides the knot back and forth on its chain, a nervous habit she has acquired over the past few years since her mother died. This necklace, a gift from her mother, is a symbol representing their family of three, but after today, that has changed.

Still sliding the knot back and forth, matching the tempo of the rocking chair, she brushes back a strand of her long blond hair and further recalls the events of the day—the warm glow of love radiating from the couple and the sparkle in Rita's eyes. A sparkle as bright as if tiny flames danced within her orbs.

Gabby thought the groom handsome. She recognized his cheekbones because she has inherited them. She watched as his strong, familiar hands slipped the gold band on Rita's fourth finger.

"You may kiss your bride." Gabby recalls the minister's words as she witnessed the start of her father's new life.

Brought back to the present moment by the night breeze, she sets her glass down on the table. Once again, she gazes up into the black night. A soothing, peaceful whisper beckons her. It comes from deep within her soul, and she remembers her mother's words.

"Look, Gabby! Look to the stars. Let them guide you. When you see their reflection in the pond, it will remind you that just as the stars high in the heavens are seen in the waters on the earth, as you wish upon a star, your dreams carried upward will come back to you."

Anna, her mother, would then point to a star, encouraging Gabby to make a wish. *"Dreams really do come true. Never forget that, my sweet daughter."* Young Gabby would snuggle closer as she sat on her mother's lap, breathing in her familiar scent.

Thinking of her mother has brought on this nostalgic feeling in the past, but this nagging feeling is different and has appeared several times today. *What's wrong with me?* She looks down at the napkin in her lap, and her eyes catch the boldly printed words, Wayne and Rita King. True, the twenty-nine-year-old Gabby had hopes of her own wedding; however, it never crossed her mind that her father would beat her to the altar. She sits back in the rocking chair and closes her eyes. Putting her mother's words into action, she touches her precious trinity knot necklace once more as she picks out a star and makes her wish.

Today her father married her boss, the owner of the art gallery in their small town. Gabby is happy they found love. Really, she is, and she feels foolish that she is allowing the nostalgia of days long past to creep from her memory, stealing her joy. Her father has taken a bold step. He is creating a new life trekking forward with a new wife by his side. *Will he forget about Anna?* Gabby wonders if she's sad because the dear memory of her mother may fade—or troubled that her daddy is doing a better job of moving forward than she.

Startling her by his touch breaking her thoughts, Brett says, "Hey! There you are. I've been looking for you." As he pushes her long blond strands to the side, his warm breath against her neck causes her to shiver. Reaching his arms around the back of the chair, he embraces her and she rests her head back and gazes up at this handsome Adonis.

Brett has a tall, muscular build, and his long, brown curly hair is accentuated by his emerald eyes, giving him quite an edge with the ladies. However, it is well-traveled news that the dashing tennis pro is currently off the market.

Gabby is an artist and a tennis player, but more importantly, she is the daughter of Wayne King, the wealthy cattle and oil baron. Her relationship with Brett surprises her and it has raised many eyebrows at the country club. In the past, she has been conservative in her choice of men, and she never dated men who were considered players. But Brett's reputation around the club has members watching to see how long it will be before Gabby becomes just another name added to his long lists of conquests. However, here it is two months into their relationship, and she is happier than she could have ever imagined and he has remained faithful.

"I just needed a break. It has been quite a day." She reaches up to pat his hand.

He briefly massages her shoulders, then leans closer and kisses her on the cheek. His hands are strong, and the tension begins to leave her muscles. His spicy scent still makes her senses reel, and she closes her eyes.

"That feels nice." She leans back farther to get a glimpse of him. "Where are the bride and groom?"

Continuing to massage her shoulders, he says, "Off to bed. It's well after midnight."

She sits up straight and puts out her lower lip. "They didn't even say good night? What's up?"

"It's their wedding night," he whispers. "They want to be alone." He laughs softly.

She's beginning to realize that she is going to have to share her father. As an only child, she has always been the center of King's attention. Would everything change now that he has remarried?

Although an adult, she still wants to be Daddy's little girl. Would Rita replace her as his favorite?

Brett breaks the silence. "I'm sure they're both exhausted. Aren't you worn out, my princess?"

This time, Gabby avoids looking up because she doesn't want him to see her tear-filled eyes. *He will think me silly.*

"Come on, let's go upstairs. Let Jamie and the caterer take care of all of this." She starts to protest, but with a swift movement he lifts her out of the rocker and gathers her in his arms. "You, Miss Gabby, are going to bed." Mesmerized, she can feel her body relaxing. She loves him more than she thought possible and she presses her head into his chest.

Up the curved stairway, he carries her to her bedroom. He lies down on the comforter next to her and strokes her face. "I don't think I have ever seen you this way."

Her heart screams inside. However, she doesn't respond and keeps her eyes closed. *It's best to keep quiet.*

"Good night, my love." His voice is soft and his kiss sweet. Reaching down, he removes her shoes and covers her with the afghan. Finally, he flips off the light and quietly closes the door.

In the darkness, Gabby silently cries.

Brett

Descending the stairway to the great room, Brett sees Rita's sons, Will and Stan, sitting around the large dining room table. They flew to Texas from the East Coast just the evening before. Will, the younger son, is tall and lean and is an accountant. Stan, at thirty-three, is four years older. Unlike his brother, Stan has broad shoulders. He started working as a motorcycle mechanic after making his fortune as an attorney in a prominent Washington, D.C., law firm.

Will, the more extroverted of the two brothers, speaks first. "Brett, come and join us."

Stan looks up, shifting his eyes as if sizing Brett up. Brett nods and pulls out a chair and sits down. With a practiced hand, Will slides a beer across the wooden table from one end to where Brett is seated.

Will says, "I guess it's official—our mother, who has always been a queen, is now married to a king."

Brett twists the cap off the bottle and takes a swig of the beer but doesn't speak.

"I like King," Will says. "I think Mom landed a good one." Then he pauses and looks to Brett as if waiting for a response.

"Yes, they're both wonderful people. It's obvious they respect each other," Brett says.

Shifting his weight in the chair, Will looks around. "I hope my mother knows what she's getting into." He gestures with his beer raised in the air. "It's nice here. Don't get me wrong, but I wouldn't give up my life in the city for this. This ranch feels like it's in the middle of nowhere."

Brett sees Stan open his mouth as if to speak, but Stan shakes his head and stays silent.

"I love the open country," Brett says. "I grew up near here on a neighboring ranch, then I left for seventeen years, but now after all that time away, I'm realizing how much I've missed it. I enjoy my time spent here."

Will holds up his beer bottle. "Better you than me. Guess that's what makes the world go around, different people like different things." He brings the bottle to his lips.

Stan says, "I kind of like it here." Both Will and Brett stare at him, and Stan changes the subject. "Brett, how long have you and Gabby been together?"

"Only a few months," Brett answers. He looks around the room to see if anyone is overhearing their conversation.

Stan sits up straighter and shakes his head from side to side. "She sure is fine, smart, good-looking, and she has a great figure." He gives a little whistle as he taps his fingers on his beer bottle.

Suddenly Brett is unable to take a deep breath, as if he has been hit in the gut. It forces him to lean forward slightly in his chair, and he stares up with his head cocked sideways, searching Stan's face to grasp the true meaning of his words. Should he be concerned that Stan might make a play for Gabby? *Play it cool. I'm probably overreacting. Stan is just stating the obvious. Stan is Gabby's step-brother now. But that really doesn't mean they can't date. I'd never thought of Rita's sons as being a threat... until now.*

These past few months, he and Gabby have just been starting to get to know one another. When they're together, it feels so right, and he can't imagine life without her. He deems himself lucky to be in a relationship with her after their big misunderstanding: he moved too fast and was too aggressive. Hiding his fears behind a screen of power, he was an arrogant playboy. But all of that is in the past. That was the old Brett. Remembering how Rita played a huge role in getting them together gives him some hope that Stan and Will realize that Gabby is off-limits. Brett feels blessed that Gabby, with her big heart, had forgiven him and he is indebted to Rita for her role in getting him a second chance.

Looking over once more toward Stan, he tries to see Stan through Gabby's eyes. Checking out Stan as a potential mate for Gabby makes him think of another man that she dated.

Richard had been Gabby's boyfriend for over two years. He had even asked her to marry him—twice, to be accurate. Richard, an attorney, is currently making a run for a seat in the U.S. Senate. He should have been a great match for Gabby. A smart man, he runs in the same circle of businessmen as Wayne King. But Richard has a flaw. He is a cheater. Brett smiles because he knows Gabby does not tolerate such behavior. No, on second thought he knows that his initial assessment was wrong, as Stan seems to be nothing like Richard. However, as he considers Stan's build and redeeming qualities, Brett is reminded of himself. Is this why he is feeling so insecure? He finishes the last swallow of his beer.

"Excuse me, boys. It was nice talking with you." Brett pushes back his chair and shakes hands with Will and then Stan. "I need to be at work tomorrow morning, so I'm going to hit the road."

He walks out the front door. From the porch, he surveys the vast open space that stretches for miles. He stands for a moment and breathes in deeply. *God, I do love it here.*

He listens to the noises of the night. A frog croaks, and a coyote howls in the distance. The lonely tone of the howl resonates to a place deep in his soul. He chuckles and shakes his head. His burden is lightened because he knows its source. His uneasiness isn't caused solely by Stan's remarks about Gabby—it started when Stan mentioned that he "liked it here." Stan has a rugged edge about him that would serve him well if he ever decided to move to Texas.

Brett also recalls last night at the wedding rehearsal. That evening, during a pre-dinner toast, King gave an open invitation to Rita's sons to visit the ranch anytime and to consider the ranch their home. King called them "family." This inclusion has given Stan a better position with the King family than he. His stomach knots.

Like Gabby, Brett was an only child and lost his mother at a young age, but he also lost his father when he was a teenager. For years, he has been without family. In these past few months, dating Gabby and coming to the ranch, he has finally felt as if he does have family. Now, his new safe haven is being threatened.

Once again he breathes in the fresh night air. As he stands staring at the open country, he feels a connection with nature. He wants wide-open spaces in his life, and seeing this countryside on horseback every day would be his fondest dream. *Am I ready for change? Maybe I should quit my tennis job or teach tennis part-time, and then ask King to take me on at the ranch.*

Thinking of work on a ranch brings back memories of his father as he taught Brett the skills necessary to be a successful cowboy. He smiles, recalling his past.

"That was better. Next time, keep your horse facing the steer at all times," said Mr. Matthews as a young Brett was learning to cut cattle, a skill necessary to separate a cow from the herd.

Later, when he was learning to rope calves, his father said, "Hold your piggin' line tight. Don't drop it. It doesn't do you any good to get a quick lasso and then have nothing to tie the calf's legs together with."

"Yes, sir," said Brett. "I'll remember."

"Son, you're getting better. You'll do me proud," Mr. Matthews said as he patted his son on the shoulders.

Yes, he remembers when his dad made him practice all of these skills. He loved the time they'd spent together. However, these times came to an end. While in high school, Brett picked up a tennis racquet and found that he had some talent, and he was offered a tennis scholarship. When his dad passed during Brett's first year at college, not only had he stopped riding and competing in rodeos but he'd also made a vow to never return to a life on a ranch.

Well, that was all before he met Gabby. Now, everything is different. Just thinking of her makes the corners of his mouth curve upward and his heart beat just a bit louder. How has she managed to invade most of his thoughts? He has never had a long-term relationship. Nor has he ever been in love. Will this feeling last? It's Gabby that makes him want to be a better man. Before her, he was lost and reckless. He drank too much, and he used women. He only cared about himself. Now, all of that has changed. He isn't alone anymore. He has family. Rita's mothering has helped him find his way. And it was Wayne King who reminded him to respect others, but more importantly, have respect for himself. Plus, meeting the Kings has forced him to face his past, thus allowing him to return to the ranch life that he had once loved.

If he did follow through on his thoughts and come to work at the ranch, it would limit the time he could spend with Gabby, because she lives in town. Maybe he could do both and split his time—teach tennis part-time on the weekends and work at the ranch during the week. He remembers that she tries to visit the ranch once a month, but her job at the gallery requires her to work some weekends. Would her work schedule change now that Rita is married to King? Would Gabby be working more weekends at the gallery so that Rita could be here at the ranch? He can see a conflict arising in their work schedules along with a change in the dynamics between the two women.

All of these thoughts of family remind him of the wedding gift Gabby presented to her dad and Rita.

"Here, open it," Gabby said proudly. Rita ripped the paper off the gift, revealing the canvas, and held the painting up for all to get a better view. Similar to Gabby's Trinity Knot series, the painting was also a knot, but this knot was a zeppelin bend. "It's called 'New Beginnings,' as the two ropes represent our two families joining together," she had explained to the family that gathered for cocktails after the wedding rehearsal.

He recalls her excitement about her new painting series. The zeppelin bend knot was perfect for her subject matter. He is sure that with all the excitement of the wedding and new family members, she hasn't given any thought to all the potential problems larger families can create, because she always sees the best in everyone and everything. That's just one of the qualities about her that he loves.

When she explained the meaning of the zeppelin bend painting, he felt that he was a part of this new beginning. However, standing here on the porch after his conversation with Rita's sons, he feels alone, an outsider. Once again he hears the coyote howl in the distance.

When is Stan leaving? Brett never thought to ask. Remembering the past two days, Stan did seem to hover near Gabby. Is his imagination running wild? He climbs into the seat of his Audi sports car. He looks around once again and shakes his head.

Yes, Brett does trust Gabby, but he doesn't trust Stan. It's unfortunate that Brett's scheduled for the morning tennis drill at the country club. He would rather stay here and protect his love interest.

Since he's feeling so unsettled, he knows sleep won't be coming soon, so he may as well drive back to the city. After taking a deep breath, his smile returns and he lifts his head and pulls back his shoulders. He slowly drives down the lane toward the main road with his convertible top down. Hitting the open road, the night air feels great as the freedom of the wind has given him the answer to his dilemma. He throws the Audi into fifth gear and his mood is lighter. *All of this can be fixed.*

CHAPTER 2

Gabby

The sun peeks through the window, shining on Gabby's face. She rolls over and checks the time. Still early, not even seven o'clock. She lifts her arms, stretches, and feels grateful for the day. Inhaling another deep breath, she stretches again. She must have been exhausted as it's unusual for her to sleep through the night. She snuggles and feels the warmth of the comforter. She glances around the room and sees the familiar artwork on the walls. These are the scenes she painted as a child and with encouragement from her mother to celebrate each birthday, and the paintings seem to return her smile.

She sits up quickly. Where is Brett? It takes her a few seconds to remember that he had plans to leave early since he had the morning shift at the tennis club. She looks over to the other side of the bed but sees no signs of him having slept there. Where did he sleep? Did he stay up to the wee hours of the day chatting and drinking with the men? She pouts because she knows that she won't see him for a few days, and she really wanted to say goodbye.

Unlike Brett, who had to work today, she can stay at the ranch for a few days. Rita has closed the art gallery for the entire week. Gabby will reopen it the following weekend when her daddy and Rita are on their honeymoon.

Hopping down the stairs, she eagerly looks for the newlyweds. Her father, always an early riser, is the only one at the table. Absorbed in reading his morning paper, he doesn't hear her approaching him from behind, and she reaches around him and gives him a hug, followed by a kiss on his gray-speckled beard.

"Hello there, kitten. How are you this morning?" He looks up over the rim of his glasses and sports a grin similar to the one a young boy might give to his grandmother after she catches him with his mouth full of cookies before dinner.

"I'm doing great. And from that smirk on your face, I gather you are doing great as well," she answers, shyly turning away so as not to reveal the redness she feels creeping up her face. "Call me selfish, but I'm glad to have you all to myself for a bit." She pulls out the chair next to him and pours a cup of coffee. "Where's Rita?"

"Taking her time like a bride should the morning after her wedding night." He sits back and winks. "While on the subject of my new wife, how do you think yesterday went?"

"I think everyone had a good time."

"Good! I think so, too," He reaches for her hand and squeezes it before planting a kiss. "I'm really glad for your support. Thanks for being there for Rita and for me. We both love you very much."

"I know, Daddy." She looks down at her lap, and the tears start to flow once again. *Darn, I'm doing it again.* "I'm sorry." She wipes a tear before it falls down her cheek.

He hugs her and draws her closer. "I'm just moving on, not forgetting, just moving forward. Your mother would want that for us... me and you."

"I know. I know. It's silly." Dabbing her eyes with a napkin, she peers up into his kind, loving face.

She wipes away another tear and sniffles as she remembers an overheard conversation between her parents just a few short weeks before Anna died.

Gabby was hidden in the doorway as she watched her daddy help her mother walk to the overstuffed chair. From their somberness, she could tell there was no good news from the doctor. She watched as her daddy tucked the afghan around his frail wife and gave her a kiss.

"Thank you, my dear. Thank you for loving me and sharing your life with me," Anna said. "God has a different plan for us. My life will soon be over, but yours will go on. Take care of yourself and our princess." Anna looked up and touched King's face. "Promise me, Wayne, that you will live your life to the fullest. Nothing will make me happier than to look down from heaven and see you and Gabby happy."

"Don't give up hope, Anna. Miracles happen. Doctors aren't always right. They make mistakes. I need you. Gabby needs you." King, the strong, fearless cowboy, knelt and held his wife and cried. After hearing these words and watching the scene playing out before her, Gabby lowered herself to the floor in disbelief.

She had never seen her daddy cry. She had always thought him invincible. It was devastating to watch his six-foot frame bent over in such anguish. As predicted, the cancer won the battle. For two years

Anna had fought that devil with numerous treatments from the best cancer research center in the nation. However, the cancer continued to grow. Anna surrendered a few weeks after the conversation Gabby had overheard.

Gabby recalls her devastation. Her grief tried to swallow her up, and seemed sure to win, but then something just short of miraculous happened. She found a voice with her brush as it cried to the canvas, and she painted the first of her Trinity Knot series. The source of this inspiration was the trinity knot necklace given to her by her mother on her sixteenth birthday. As the series expanded, depicting the knot became a source of healing. Since then, whenever she is anxious or thinking about her mother, she unconsciously swings the familiar knot back and forth on its chain. She is doing it now as her daddy holds her hand.

Their quiet time is interrupted when Stan and Will amble down the stairs to join them.

"Good morning," Will says as he pulls out a chair across from King.

Stan touches Gabby on the shoulder before sitting down next to her. He must have sensed the solemn mood as he starts talking and sharing a joke he had heard at the wedding. Before long, she is laughing with the rest of them. Meanwhile, Rita has also joined them.

Looking around the table, Gabby sees her new family. It has more than doubled, and she smiles. With more guests seated, Jamie, the ranch foreman's wife, pours freshly brewed coffee. Her full-bodied figure alerts all that she is an excellent cook, and her huge smile reveals that she enjoys having guests to appreciate her efforts. The table sports family-sized bowls of scrambled eggs, bacon, and fresh fruit.

"Wow, this is great," Will says.

"Glad you like it. The best is yet to come," Jamie proudly boasts as she walks back to the kitchen.

Within a few minutes, Jamie returns carrying a large platter of her signature blueberry pancakes and places it in front of Gabby.

Gabby's eyes light up. "My favorite."

Jamie leans down and whispers, "I thought you might need a little TLC this morning."

"Thank you," Gabby says. "You always know how to make me feel special."

Jamie and Rusty are the ranch caretakers. Rusty has been working for King for more than two decades as foreman. When Anna died, King started to split his time between the ranch and his condo downtown, so he invited the couple to move into the ranch house. Working as a team, Jamie takes care of the household, and Rusty takes charge of the cattle and supervises the ranch hands. Gabby has known them almost all her life and considers them family.

Jamie reaches into her apron pocket, pulls out a folded piece of paper, and slips it into Gabby's hand.

She knits her brow. "What's this?"

Jamie pats her on the shoulder and whispers once again, "A handsome young man asked me to give it to you."

"When did he leave, Jamie?" she asks as she holds onto Jamie's arm.

"He left last night. You were already asleep. He thought you would be concerned because he originally planned to go back to town early this morning. He didn't want to wake you."

Gabby lowers her eyes and opens the note as she holds it under the table.

Gabby,

So sorry I left without getting a chance to tell you goodbye. The conditions were perfect for a night drive with the top down. I'll miss you terribly. I love you.

Call me,

Brett

A smile crosses her face at his thoughtfulness. She does miss him and wishes he could be here with the rest of her family. She looks up, suddenly aware that all seated at the table are staring at her.

"Gabby, what do you say?" King asks, staring at his daughter.

"I'm so sorry. I wasn't paying attention."

He repeats his question. "How about showing Will and Stan around?"

Will pipes up quickly, "Sorry, Wayne, or should I call you Dad?" He pauses and laughs. "But I have a conference call this morning. Even though I would really like to join you on a tour of the ranch, work comes first."

Stan says, "I want to see it. That is, if it's okay with you, Gabby?"

"Of course, I would love to show you. It will be fun." She sees Stan smiling and thinks he has a kind face.

King excuses himself. "Speaking of work, I need to get moving. I have lots to handle before going on my honeymoon." Rita's beaming face looks up at him, and he leans over to kiss his bride. "See y'all at dinner tonight."

Rita stands. "I'll walk you out." She places her arm around his waist. Seeing their mutual smiles, Gabby feels a streak of jealousy.

She knows her daddy's routine well. He will saddle up Monster, his brown quarter horse, and ride to the pastures with Rusty. Taking advantage of the cooler morning temperatures, the two men will cover the land where the cattle are grazing. After lunch as the sun is high in the sky, they will switch from horseback to an all-terrain vehicle and continue to survey and take inventory of as much of the remaining three hundred thousand acres as possible.

She also knows that her daddy does not take his wealth for granted, as she has watched him work long, hard hours. In addition to his strong work ethic, King is a man of great integrity. The combination of these two qualities has brought him respect as a valued citizen in the community. She not only loves him dearly but she respects him as well. She doesn't wish him to spend the rest of his days alone. It's good that he and Rita are together.

She turns her attention back to Stan. "Do you like to ride? It's the best way to see the ranch."

He moves nervously in his chair. "I'll take a raincheck on horseback riding." Shifting his eyes downward, he clears his throat. "I've never been."

She smiles. "You should try. It'll be fun. It's easy, and I'll teach you everything you need to know. When you get tired, we'll switch over to the Jeep. How does that sound?"

"I'm willing to give it a try. Are you sure you are up to teaching an old guy?"

"Stop it! You're not that old,"

Will chuckles. "Yes, he is."

Stan raises his eyes and glares at his brother. "Bet this old man can beat the crap out of you. Want to take it outside?"

"Boys, I thought you were past that silly sibling rivalry stuff," Rita yells as she comes back to the dining room, hands on her hips.

"I knew it was too good to be true. You're showing Gabby your true colors. What is she to think?"

"I never had a brother or a sister," Gabby says, "so I think it's fun to hear them tease each other." She looks from Will to Stan and then back again. "It's the perfect day for a ride. Will, are you sure you can't go with us?"

"Another time. I really need to be on this conference call. It could last two hours or so. Besides, you'll have your hands full with this guy." Will nods his head in Stan's direction.

She notices that Will is quieter this morning than when he first came to the ranch. She knows that he spent most of his time with Ella at the wedding reception. Ella and Gabby have been best friends since their sorority days at the University of Texas. In contrast to Gabby's tall stature, straight blond hair and conservative nature, Ella is short with curly brunette hair that she keeps cut in a chic style and is extremely outgoing and impulsive.

Last evening after many of the guests had departed, she saw Ella and Will in a long embrace on the far side of the porch. It was the sound of Ella's familiar giggle that gave Gabby the sense that the couple was moving fast. She is happy for Ella if, indeed, she and Will hit it off; however, she wishes Ella would learn to coast in first gear and get to know him before speeding out of control. Ella has been known to fall in love overnight.

Gabby recalls sitting on the couch with her friend in their sorority house years ago.

"There, there, Ella. He isn't worth all of your tears," Gabby said.

"But I love him. I thought he loved me." Ella sobbed. *"We were great*

together." Her shoulders dropped, and her head hung low as tears rolled down her cheeks.

"Here's a tissue. Blow your nose. There's a man out there for you. It just isn't this one." Gabby held Ella in her arms and rocked her, just like Gabby's mother used to hold her.

With Ella, first there was Robert, and then Jason, Dan, and Matt...well, over the past years there were too many men for Gabby to remember. Ella's list of heartbreaks is long. More recently, Richard and Brett also got their names on the list. First, Ella made it known to everyone at the country club that she wanted Brett. Then, after she saw Gabby with Brett, she cried to Gabby, voicing her hurt and betrayal. Gabby remembers her words clearly. "Why did you take him when you knew I wanted him?" Later, Gabby's former boyfriend's name was added to the list, but Ella was devastated when she realized that the extent of her relationship with Richard was a one-night stand.

Gabby rolls her eyes. She loves Ella's free spirit but doesn't understand why Ella never learns that her reckless behavior leads to the same destructive outcome. Would she be comforting her friend again after Will left? Maybe this time it would be different, and her new step-brother would be the man Ella has been searching for. Nonetheless, if Will is just another heartbreak waiting to happen, Ella can count on Gabby to help her pick up the shattered pieces of her life.

CHAPTER 3

Gabby

Later that morning as they walk to the barn, Stan reaches over and places his arm around Gabby's waist. She moves away, but he readjusts his hold. Stan is just a few inches taller than she. His dark brown hair shows signs of thinning and his matching brown eyes are framed with crow's feet on the corners, giving him the appearance of someone wise. In addition, his wide shoulders warn of muscles hidden under his shirt. Stan would be a man to reckon with in a fight.

"Thank you so much for showing me around. I've never spent any time on a ranch before, but I can tell that I like it here." He looks out into the distant horizon. "My mother must also like it here because she seems happier than I have seen her in many years. She went through a rough patch raising Will and me after our dad died." He tells her a little about how things were in those first gloomy months.

"I remember one day when Will and I were going to the park and I asked her to come with us," he says. "She answered, 'No, you go on ahead,' and waved her arm in the air as if shooing us out of the door.

I told her, 'You've been in the house for weeks. The sun is shining. We'll walk around the lake, take a blanket, and have a picnic lunch. You love picnics.'

"Mother still said no, and I got down on my knees and took her hand. 'Fresh air and sunshine. It will be good for you. Please come,' I begged. She said, 'Look at me. I'm a mess. I'm not even dressed,' and she straightened her robe and fussed with her hair.

"I said, 'Mother, you've been moping around for months. It's time to stop grieving. Okay?' and she screamed, 'Don't tell me how I should feel!' She saw the hurt in my eyes and quickly said, 'I'm so sorry, honey. I can't, not yet. Please understand.' Both of us were crying."

Stan assures Gabby that his mother's remarriage has made him very happy.

"Mother speaks very highly of you and your father. I'm glad to be able to spend some time getting to know y'all better." He laughs. "Did I say that with the right accent?"

"You did just fine. I'll give you a tip." Gabby stops walking and faces him with her hands on her hips. "If you hang around my dad long enough, he'll turn you into a Texan, and you won't even realize until you look in the mirror someday and wonder, how did that happen?" She slaps her thigh and starts walking again. "Is that what you want?"

"I could get used to living here." He nods. "To answer your question, yes."

"Well, let's get started. I'd better teach you how to ride. You can't be a Texan and not know how to ride."

As they round the corner to the barn, Rusty meets them at the stable. He has Frog and Lady saddled for their ride.

She gives Rusty a wave. "I'm surprised to see you here. I thought you would be out with Daddy."

"I'm meeting him in the east pasture where the cattle are grazing, after I get the two of you on your way," Rusty says.

Stan shifts his feet from side to side in the dirt. "Just a reminder, I've never done this before." He shakes his head and takes in a deep breath.

She slaps him on the back. "There's no time like the present. It's good to learn new things. It's easy. You'll see." She reaches up to the brown mare. "Lady's my horse. She's really gentle. You can ride her. Come and meet her."

Stan takes a small step toward Lady.

"Lady," Gabby says, "this is Stan. Say hello." Lady lowers her head toward Gabby, who puts her cheek against the mare's cheek. Stan reaches his hand out to touch the horse's nose. Lady flares her nostrils and snorts. He quickly jumps back.

Gabby giggles. "She won't bite. Lady's looking for her treat. I always bring her one."

She hands an apple to Stan. "Hold it in the palm of your hand with your fingers extended. You'll make a friend for life. Lady loves apples."

He cautiously moves his hand toward Lady, but before he can get close, Lady quickly grabs the apple with her lips. He nervously leans back, startled by the horse's sudden movement.

Gabby laughs again. "I'm so sorry. I'm not laughing to make you feel bad." She touches his arm. "There's nothing to worry about. She's a doll. You both need to get to know one another."

She lovingly gives Lady another pat. Suddenly, Frog snorts, and he rubs Lady with his nose. "Okay, okay, yes, I have one for you too." A brown quarter horse with a white mane, Frog is a hand taller than Lady.

"They act like children. You've got to treat them the same or their feelings get hurt." She feeds Frog an apple, then pats him. "You feel better now?" She turns her attention back to Stan. "Frog is a great horse, and he's a hard worker."

With instructions and much encouragement, Stan is finally in the saddle. She shows him how to hold the reins and how to turn Lady to the right and left. She also shows him how to nudge Lady using his knees.

"This is so intimidating." He raises his eyes to meet hers.

"You'll be fine. Really, just relax."

"I wish I was as sure as you."

After some practice riding around the dirt path near the barn, he seems to be getting the hang of it.

She rides next to him. "You ready to give this a try?"

"Ready as I'll ever be."

Gabby, riding Frog, heads down the trail that follows the creek to the lake. Without any help from Stan, Lady follows closely behind them. On this beautiful April day, the sun is shining, and the Texas wildflowers are at their best. Bluebonnets fill the meadows, with some Indian paintbrush scattered throughout, and pink primrose line the edges of the trail.

"This is my favorite time of year," she calls over her shoulder. "I love all of the flowers."

Stan has a puzzled look. "Did you plant them?"

She smiles, aware that she has laughed and giggled far too often about the things he has said or done.

"No, they grow wild here," she uses her most matter-of-fact voice.

"Amazing. It's beautiful."

They meander down the path several more minutes.

"How are you doing?" She looks back at Stan and Lady again. "Is horseback riding what you envisioned? It's easy, right?"

"Much easier than I imagined. It seems that Lady is just following Frog. I'm not doing much of anything." He smiles.

"She knows Frog needs to be the boss, so she lets him lead. I told you she's smart."

A few moments later, she hears a noise. *What's wrong?* At first, glancing behind her, she's confused. Lady is rearing up on her hind legs, and her front legs are high in the air. Stan holds on to the reins but loses his footing in the stirrups, and he starts to lean to the left. She hears the rattle of the snake before she sees it on the trail. She quickly dismounts Frog and goes back to help Stan. Before she can get to them, he falls off Lady and lands on his butt. The commotion causes the snake to slither off the trail and into the high grass near the creek.

Lady, still obviously upset, is nervously turning right and left.

"It's okay, girl. It's okay. He's gone." She manages to grab the dangling reins. After quieting Lady, she can focus on Stan. "How about you? Are you hurt?"

"I'm not sure just yet. Let me see if I can get up."

She reaches out her hand to help pull him up to a standing position, but he is too heavy.

"Wait, wait, I can do it," he says. Carefully, he gets up on all fours and finally stands upright, and he starts to brush the dirt off his jeans. "I didn't see that one coming."

"I'm so sorry. Lady hates snakes, but I guess telling you that now is a little too late."

"She's not the only one," he mutters under his breath.

"I'm really sorry. It rarely happens. Honest. But this time of the year as the flowers bloom, the rattlesnakes are more prevalent." She brushes the dust off Stan's back. "Horses and snakes don't make the best of friends."

"I'm glad the snake decided to go away, and no one was bitten." He looks in the direction where he last saw the snake slither into the tall grass.

"Are you sure you're okay?" she asks again, looking him over.

"Just my pride is injured, I think." He grins at her.

"I'm glad that you didn't break a bone or hit your head on a rock when you fell. Never let go of the reins or lose your hold in the stirrups."

"Now you tell me." He wipes his brow.

"You'll have a great story to tell, along with the bruises you'll be sporting tomorrow." She pats him on the back.

"I'm quite sure I won't be showing anyone my butt, no matter how awesome the bruise."

"The best thing right now for you would be to get back on the horse. However, that's easier said than done." She raises her eyebrows. "That snake sure is lucky."

He looks skeptical and scratches his head. "How do you figure that?"

"If my dad were here, he would have shot it."

Stan motions toward the grass where the snake escaped. "So what happens to the snake? We just let it go?" His voice quivers.

"Pretty much," she says. "It was rare to see it on the trail. Usually, they feel the vibration from the horses' hooves and stay clear."

She senses that Stan is still shaken from his fall. "Since we're close to the barn, let's walk back, and we'll drive the Jeep. Sound good?"

He nods.

They lead their horses by the reins. After a few minutes, Stan speaks. "Glad I fell on my ass—lots of padding back there." He brushes more of the dirt off his jeans and looks around. "It sure is beautiful here, even if you do have snakes. I never spent any time in the hill country. We lived all over when my dad was in the Army. After he died, we lived in the city until I left for college."

Arriving back at the barn, he continues. "Then I landed a job in D.C. and little brother followed me there. We've lived there now for four years."

"You must like it, right?" she says.

"It's comfortable and familiar."

She takes off her hat and wipes her brow with her shirt sleeve. "I've always lived here. Well, mostly. A few years ago, I went to New York City to market my art. It didn't go well. I didn't sell enough to pay my rent. Besides, my dad was lonely. I was lonely." She reaches for her trinity knot necklace. "It was time to come back. That's when I applied for a job at your mother's art gallery." She looks at Stan for a reaction. "I'm really grateful she hired me and gave me wall space for my art."

He smiles. "Mother says that she's really grateful you came to her shop." He gives Gabby a nudge with his elbow. "She has always loved art. She dabbles a bit, but she doesn't have the talent that you have."

Gabby glares at him. "You've seen my art?" She can't remember discussing her art career since he arrived.

He grins. "Your wedding gift…the Zeppelin Bend."

Feeling foolish, she giggles. "Of course, how silly of me." She brushes her hair back from her face.

Stan adds, "I would love to see more. That is, if you wouldn't mind."

They walk into the corral, and she ties the horses' reins to the fence before she fetches some water. She pours it into the trough.

"Will and I have yet to visit Art Smart," he says. "Maybe we can stop on our way back to the airport." He shifts his weight from side to side. "Are you coming back to town with us?"

"Yes, I am. I'm managing the gallery while Rita and Daddy are on their honeymoon." She looks away. *Honeymoon.* It is the first time she has spoken the word aloud. Her stomach churns and that gnawing sadness creeps over her again. *Really, Gabby? Get over it!*

Taking a deep breath, she turns and runs into the barn to grab the keys to the Jeep. She comes out twirling them around her finger. Stan is staring out into the horizon.

"Come on, Stan. Let's go for a ride. You're driving." She throws him the keys.

"I'll give you directions as we go." She secures her hair in a ponytail with an elastic band. "You up for this?" she calls to him as she walks around the barn.

"Oh, yeah!" His face is beaming. She sighs in relief as she knows from that smile and the tone of his voice that his fall is not foremost on his mind. He runs to catch up with her.

She says, "I would have been disappointed if you said no." The Jeep is parked on the side of the barn, and they crawl in. Stan starts the engine and revs it up a few times.

"I never want to disappoint a pretty lady," He winks and buckles his seat belt. "This will be great. If I see that rattler, I'm gonna run him over." He pushes his foot down hard on the accelerator.

The next few hours go by quickly as they tour the ranch—the oil fields, the pastures full of longhorn cattle, and the lake. They wave and beep the horn at King and Rusty down by the eastern fence as they zoom by, kicking up dust. With the sun high in the sky and the temperature warm, she's glad she grabbed some water out of the refrigerator in the barn. She enjoys the wind hitting her face and, as expected, Stan is a great driver. After all, he's a mechanic! When the Jeep's gauge shows a low gas level, it forces them return to the barn.

She has enjoyed herself. Stan is easy to be with. He's average in looks, but his dry sense of humor makes her laugh. He's also bright and the more acquainted she becomes with him, the more she is beginning to see his inner charm. He's always the gentlemen and very attentive. He never failed to assist her in and out of the Jeep.

He's probably just being nice since we are family now. Am I silly to think his gestures suggest something more? Clearly, Stan knows that I'm with Brett. However, there's that sparkle in his eye whenever he looks at me. I must be careful. I don't want to give him the wrong impression.

Her thoughts are broken by Stan's concerned voice. "I noticed the lights on the dash flickered, and the engine missed at times. It feels like your Jeep may have a loose frame ground. If you have some tools, I can take care of that." He raises the hood of the Jeep and disappears under it for a few seconds.

"Rusty can get you some tools when he comes back," she says. "I'm not sure where they're kept. But he won't be back until later."

"Good, that will give the engine a chance to cool down a bit." He looks up and flashes her a grin and then slams the hood down

Suddenly, with no advance notice, a wave of nausea sweeps over her. *Am I going to lose my breakfast?* His driving was fast but careful, just the opposite of her experience with Brett behind the wheel. If she were to have motion sickness, that ride would have done it, not this one. She takes a few deep breaths and places her hand on her stomach, waiting for the feeling to pass.

"You okay?" he asks.

"I'm fine," she lies.

Relieved that her nausea has lessened, she exits the shade of the barn with Stan and they walk toward the house. She shields her eyes from the sun as she wipes her brow. "I'm going to skip lunch."

The corners of his mouth turn downward, and she can feel his disappointment.

"Is it something I did?" He scratches his head and looks at her with puppy-dog eyes.

"No, no...I guess I haven't recovered from yesterday. The wedding was a busy time, and I think I drank too much wine." She pauses as if thinking. "Maybe I am a little dehydrated from being out in the sun. A couple of glasses of water should do the trick. Besides, did you see all of those scrumptious pancakes I ate this morning? I know you must be starving. Jamie will be waiting for you inside with a fabulous lunch. She'll be very disappointed if you decline."

He opens the front door for her and brushes her back ever so slightly as she passes. The gesture sends a shiver up her spine.

"There you are!" Rita calls from the kitchen. "We've been wondering where you were. We thought of sending a search party." She comes into the dining room with her hands on her hips. "You've been gone for hours. We left several messages on both your phones. However, I know that the cell phone service is a little lacking out here, so finally, Jamie got through to Rusty."

"Mother, you're always worrying," Stan says.

Rita approaches them, wringing her hands. "That's what mothers do."

He gives his mother a hug and kisses her on the cheek. "I'm sorry. We didn't think to check our phones. We had so much fun. Well…after the rattlesnake, and after I fell off the horse, and—"

"You what?" Will calls from his chair at the table. "Did you say you fell off the horse?" Will rolls his eyes and shakes his head. "I told you that you were too old for this cowboy thing."

He snickers and then chuckles.

Stan walks over to the chair and grips down hard on Will's shoulders.

"Ouch!" Will shrieks as he tries to wriggle away. However, Stan does not seem to let up.

"Boys," Rita yells. She then looks at Gabby. "I thought they would have outgrown this behavior, but I guess not."

Gabby grabs a glass of water. "Jamie, I'm passing on lunch. I ate too many of your awesome pancakes this morning. Enjoy," she calls over her shoulder as she reaches the staircase, exiting the room before any more questions are asked. Another wave of nausea hits.

She puts her back to the closed door of her bedroom and takes another deep breath. She finishes her water and scans the room before she closes her eyes. *The sun has really worn me out. Or was it Stan?* She recalls his fall and shakes her head. No one has ever fallen off a horse out on the trail. Removing her boots and taking her hair out of the ponytail, she flops on the bed and cuddles under her homemade crocheted afghan and falls asleep.

It's almost time for dinner. How could she have slept so long…so soundly? She looks at her cell phone. There are four missed calls and two text messages from Brett.

"Shoot." *How could I have forgotten?* Remembering he had asked her to call in the note Jamie handed her at breakfast, she quickly dials his number. She exhales and bites her nails as the call goes to his voice mail. "Leave a message."

"I was out showing Stan the ranch. Then I slept for a few hours. I must have been recovering from the wedding. Call me back." She hesitates and then adds, "I'm sorry." She pauses. "I love you." She also gets her fingers dancing to reply to his text. It wasn't like her to ignore her phone. However, it *definitely* wasn't like her to ignore Brett. *He'll understand, right?*

As Gabby starts down the curved staircase, her eyes meet Stan's. He gets up from the couch where he was reading a book and quickly skips across the room to stand at the bottom of the stairs. He grins.

"You sleep well?" he asks.

Embarrassed over her long nap, she looks away. "Yes, I did. I feel much better."

He stands in front of her, forcing her to stop. She sees the sparkle in his eyes and senses his joy. It looks like he has a secret and will burst if he does not share.

She searches his face with his boyish grin and knows that she must ask. "And…what have you been doing?"

His smile widens and he puffs out his chest. "I've been out riding."

"Oh, really—with whom?" She has to restrain the giggle she feels rising in her throat.

"Will…and your dad," His voice is firm and confident. "It was great. No snakes!" He chuckles. "You should have seen me." He pauses as if waiting for praise. "I was much better than Will. I'm really getting the hang of it. You'll see when we go riding again tomorrow."

She smiles. Stan is acting like a proud little boy. "Why didn't you wake me? I would have loved to have gone."

"Jamie and Rita agreed that it was best to let you rest."

Wow, is it that obvious? What's wrong with me?

Hearing laughter from the front porch, she turns in that direction.

"Want to go out and join the family? It's beautiful out there. The air is warm and the sounds of the birds—well, I don't get any of this in the city." He offers her his arm.

Her stomach rumbles. The aroma of Jamie's cooking scents the air. *Oh, yes, I skipped lunch.* She scans the porch. Rita and her daddy are seated next to each other, and her dad is holding Rita's hand. She knows this familiar gesture since she watched him hold her mother's hand this same way on this very porch. She bites her lip, and her hand touches her necklace. The sound of Will chuckling breaks her thoughts. Standing on the far end of the porch, he is on his cell phone.

Will catches her stare and smiles back, and then he says into the phone, "Gabby says hello." *It must be Ella on the other end who is causing Will to act so jovial.* Gabby waves to him.

Reminded of Brett, Gabby checks her cell. There are no new calls and or texts since she left her message. The screen remains blank. *Where is he? Why hasn't he returned my message?* She makes an excuse and walks down the steps and follows the path to the barn. She dials

Brett's number again. Once more, her call goes to his voice mail. This time, she doesn't leave a message. Hearing steps behind her on the gravel, she stops and turns.

"Is something wrong?" Stan asks as he catches up to her.

"No, everything is fine. I was just trying to reach Brett before we sit down to dinner. Daddy doesn't allow phones at the table, and I don't want to miss his call."

"Oh, okay." He looks away, so she looks down at her phone again. *Was that disappointment I heard in Stan's voice?*

He says, "I really enjoyed today. And as the saying goes, if you fall off a horse, get back on again. That's just what I did." He beams again. "I had so much fun today. Thanks again for teaching me."

"You're welcome."

Gabby is beginning to feel annoyed with him. *He follows me everywhere? Can't he tell that I want some privacy?* Not wishing to hurt his feelings, she keeps her mouth shut and reluctantly puts her phone back in her pocket. *He'll be gone in a few days. This is all new to him. He's excited and wants to share. I get it. I'll talk to Brett later.*

She turns her attention to Stan. "It's soon time for dinner." They turn around and walk back to the ranch house, but after a few steps, he reaches his arm around her waist. *Should I stop him?*

Quickening her step, she is grateful to get in sight of the others.

Her dad yells, "There you are. It's time for dinner, and I'm starved."

Stan releases his grip. Gabby looks up to the west as the sun is starting to make its descent. As she looks back toward the house she sees a figure walking toward her. Even though her eyes haven't adjusted, she recognizes that familiar walk. It is Brett.

"Hello," he yells, hastening his step. Ignoring Stan, Brett pulls

Gabby in for a hug and a kiss. She closes her eyes and inhales his spicy scent.

"This is a surprise. Why are you here?" She cocks her head to the side and looks up at him.

"I just got here a few minutes ago. When you didn't call me back, I thought something was wrong. I left work as soon as I could." He shifts his weight. "And I rescheduled a few lessons that I had on the books for tomorrow, so I'm all yours." He opens his arms wide.

She starts to speak, but he interrupts. "I've been doing a lot of thinking ..." His voice trails off. She sees Stan staring at Brett. "We'll talk about it later," Brett says quietly as if for only her ears to hear.

Stan must have gotten the message as he pushes on ahead of them.

Brett hugs her and pulls her in tight. "Did you miss me?" His eyes are pleading.

"Of course, silly." She smiles. He appears to be relieved. *Is he jealous? Why are men so insecure?*

He picks her up off her feet and swings her in the air. She giggles and holds on tightly.

"Tell me you're happy I'm here." He allows her feet to hit the ground.

She nuzzles closer. "It's wonderful—a very nice surprise."

"Hey, you two lovebirds, my dinner is getting cold," King bellows from the porch.

Gabby waves to her dad. She notices that Stan stopped at the steps to the porch and is staring off into the horizon.

"Stan, come along." Gabby puts her free arm around Stan's shoulder. "Nobody makes Daddy wait for dinner."

All three form a single line and walk up the steps to the house.

Brett, who is bringing up the rear, taps Gabby's butt. She stops midstep, and he kisses her on the cheek. A warm, contented feeling moves through her body. Yes, she is very glad that he came back to the ranch.

After dinner, Brett takes Gabby by the hand. "Come," he says, with urgency in his voice. "We need to talk."

"What's wrong?" She searches his face for a clue.

"It's not about what's wrong; it's about what's right." He flashes his dimple. She can't resist and reciprocates with a broad smile.

He leads her out of the house, down the steps, and heads toward the barn. She raises an eyebrow. "Where are we going?" she asks.

"You'll find out." He's obviously enjoying the mystery in her voice.

The noises of the night are beginning to sound like an orchestra tuning their instruments before starting their song. Feeling the cool and refreshing breeze, she looks to the sky and sees that Venus is already shining brightly. She loves this time of the evening.

As they round the side of the barn, Brett backs her up to the wall and places his arms on both sides, trapping her. His eyes sparkle. A few seconds pass before he leans toward her and kisses her passionately. Her eyes close, and her tension leaves. She has missed him, and it feels wonderful to be close.

"I love you," he says as he backs away and studies her face.

"I love you, too." Her response is quick.

He takes her face in his hands. "Gabby, listen to me. I really love you. Do you hear what I'm saying to you?" His eyes dart back and forth, seeking access into her soul.

She opens her mouth to speak, but nothing comes out. Her eyes rapidly scan his expression, searching for another clue.

"I know it has only been two months." He strokes her face. "Missing you today was driving me crazy. I want to be with you. I've never felt like this before. I need you, Gabby." He places his arm against the wall again and looks down. "Let's move in together. What do you say? Your place? My place? Anything you want, I just want to be with you."

She is wide-eyed in disbelief. Any girl would be crazy to say no to Brett. Why is she holding back?

"Say something, anything..." His eyes still sparkle, and his dimple is more pronounced.

"Isn't this sort of sudden?" She draws in her upper lip. "We're just getting to know each other. I just broke up with Richard and now..." She looks down. She doesn't wish to see his disappointment.

"If we love each other, does time really matter? If it's right, it's right. Well, it feels right to me. Does it feel right to you?" His tone is becoming desperate.

She scans his clear green eyes and gives a nervous giggle. "Who would have thought? The dashing tennis playboy wants to settle down." She pinches his cheek and tries to make light of the conversation.

"Come on, Gabby. Can you be serious? You do that to me. It's you, Gabby." He lifts her chin.

"Brett, let me think about it, okay? You caught me by surprise." She sees the gleam in his eyes is gone, so she smiles up at him and says, "It could be a good idea." She puts her finger up to her chin as if in thought.

His face remains serious. "When can I expect an answer?"

"How about soon?" she says in a teasing tone, doing her best to make light of the conversation.

He looks at her, and his face softens. "Soon isn't soon enough, but I'll respect your wishes." He kisses her again, and this time, she doesn't show any restraint. Her head leans back against the barn, and his body presses against her. She feels that he is aroused. He takes her hand and leads her around to the door and they disappear into the dark barn.

"I know the ranch hands are gone for the day," he says with a grin. "It's just you and me." He picks her up and carries her to the hay bales. He manages to undo the twine on one of the bales, and he spreads the hay around.

"What will Rusty think?"

Brett has a fast reply. "He'll think that someone made a bed, and he'd be right. Romantic, don't you think?"

She laughs aloud. "We can't do this here."

"I don't see why not. I've missed you so much." His fingers stroke her long blond hair. "Besides, it seems you need a little encouragement to help you make the right decision about us moving in together."

He lies down next to her, and their bodies mold together. He kisses her eyelids and reaches up under her skirt. His hands are warm and firm, and she can feel her breathing quicken. She giggles before reaching down and stopping his hand.

"You aren't playing fair," she says.

"Let me see if I can help you make a decision." He winks. "I've missed you so much." He rubs her back and kisses her before he reaches up under her skirt again. She giggles and pulls him in closer.

"You still aren't playing fair." She wraps his brown locks around her finger.

"All's fair in love, right?" he whispers in her ear. He reaches down and unbuckles her belt. "I want this, Gabby. I want *us*. Make love to me." He lifts her hips and slides her jeans down. Then he unzips his fly.

This time, she doesn't push his hand away. Every cell in her body is anxious for his deliberate and tender moves. Her heart beats with a quick rhythm. She wants him. She moans, and her rapid breathing matches his. She senses his hunger and responds. However, there is a nagging voice inside her head that she can't ignore. *Am I as special as he says or has he used these lines before with others? I want to believe him. My heart wants to believe him,*

Afterward, they lie, enjoying each other with an occasional light kiss or caress. Her head is on his chest, and their hearts seem to beat in unison. She closes her eyes, and she prays, thanking God for bringing her this man. *Yes, this is real. He really does love me.*

CHAPTER 4

Gabby

Gabby holds her breath and looks out the window, trying to find a distraction from the action happening below. Why is she so cold? She's lying here in a thin gown with the air conditioning blowing over her. Her feet are in the stirrups with her knees parted, and her butt is on the edge of the table. The drape prevents her from seeing; however, she is aware that the movements of the doctor and the nurse are synchronized as if doing a dance. Each move is anticipated, and they do not speak. She hears the clang of the instruments and then feels them inside her. *God, I hate this.* She closes her eyes.

"We're finished here," the doctor finally says, removing his latex gloves and turning off the lamp. He scoots his stool away from the examining table. Meanwhile, the nurse helps Gabby to a sitting position.

"Well, Mrs. King," the doctor says, "congratulations. I would guess you to be approximately ten weeks along."

"Are you sure?" she asks in a small voice, staring at him with disbelieving eyes.

The doctor continues, "With two missed menstrual cycles and a positive confirmation from the blood test, this examination confirms what I already suspected." He stops talking and flips through a chart. "Your baby should arrive at the end of October." He looks at her again, then grabs the calendar. "Let's give you a date. Yes," he says, "let's say October 27. That sounds like a fine day for a birthday."

Gabby wrings her hands. She is further along in her pregnancy than she previously thought—ten weeks. *Wow! How could I not have noticed?*

"I'll let you get dressed, and then you can meet me in my office." The doctor stands and leaves the room with the nurse following behind him.

After the door is closed, Gabby says aloud, "Oh my God! This can't be—ten weeks, ten weeks."

She sees a calendar on the counter next to the sink, grabs it and starts counting backward, flipping through the months. It is confirmed. She must have gotten pregnant the last week of January. It must have been the night after her art show reception. However, she and Brett have only been dating since Valentine's Day. She puts her hand to her mouth and gasps as she remembers that January night.

Not a word was spoken in the car on their way home after her art reception. While unlocking the door to their condo, Richard demanded with a hard look, "Tell me why you are encouraging that lowlife."

Gabby took off her jacket and flung it over the back of the couch before answering. "Brett offered to help clean up. It wasn't a big deal."

Richard grabbed her arm and turned her to face him.

"He can't be trusted." he cupped her face in his hand before continuing, "However, Gabriella, can I trust you?"

She felt his hand reach under her tank top, and he grabbed her breast firmly.

"Get undressed," he demanded.

She stood still.

"I said, get undressed." This time he expressed more authority.

She stared at him with her head cocked in disbelief. Her arm hurt under his firm grasp. He got in her face. "If you want to act like a whore, I'll treat you like one." He pushed her in the direction of their bedroom. "You can leave the heels on but nothing else."

Afterward, as Richard lay snoring next to her, she studied his face. She used to cherish this face; however, tonight, her lower lip quivered, and her heart wept. When did their love fade?

She had thought she could forgive him after his first affair, but then it happened again. She closed her eyes and shook her head as she recalled Richard's words about trust. No, she hadn't trusted Richard in over a year. The relationship that used to be close to perfect, with time, had deteriorated to something less than tolerable.

She started to dream with her eyes open. She dreamt of romance. No, Richard was not the man who made her heart sing. Closing her eyes, she saw him. She imagined how Brett's touch would feel. She saw his green eyes and his smile enhanced with a dimple. He scared her, this man. She heard quick, rapid breathing and realized that it was her own. Sleep escaped her. Gabby quietly slid out of bed and took comfort in front of her canvas with brush in hand. She confided in the canvas as if it were her best friend.

The knock at the door brings her back to the present reality.

"Are you dressed?" the nurse asks. "Dr. White is waiting for you in his office."

"Not quite," Gabby answers as she hurries to zip up the back of her dress. Her hands are shaking, and the zipper won't budge. "Give me a minute."

Minutes later, she drags her feet down the hallway. Her eyes dart back and forth, scanning for any recognizable face, but she sees none. She sighs in relief as she enters the small office.

"There you are. Have a seat," Dr. White says, looking up from the chart in front of him, and he places his pen down on the desk.

"Come in. Come in and take a seat," he says, motioning toward the empty chair.

"In another month, I would like to schedule a sonogram. It's routine. I want to make sure everything is progressing normally. If Mr. King would like to join us, we will be hearing the heartbeat." Dr. White leans back in his chair. "Sometimes, especially for the father, the pregnancy takes on—well, let's just say a new life—after he hears the heartbeat." The doctor chuckles and explains further. "Having something tangible makes first-time fathers know the pregnancy is real."

He leans forward, picks up his pen, and starts writing on the chart again. "By then, we may be able to determine the sex. Some couples want to know the sex of their child and others do not. Think about it and talk it over. I don't need to know your decision until the day of the sonogram. Of course, I'll know the sex, but I can keep a secret." He chuckles again, and Gabby notices that he seems to really enjoy his job. However, this does not ease the nervous energy she's trying to hide.

She feels slightly dizzy with this talk about Mr. King, the father, and the baby. She needs to get out of there.

"I think I'm going to be sick." She clutches her stomach.

"Around the corner to your left." He motions with his hand and without looking up. "This happens all the time the first three months. I'll write you a prescription."

Once in the bathroom, Gabby retches over the toilet. In the mirror a pale face stares back at her as she wipes her face with a cool towel. She must be having a nightmare. *I wish I would wake up. I need to wake up.* Another wave of nausea hits her. This is not a dream; this is a harsh reality.

After she comes out of the bathroom, the nurse hands her a prescription slip as well as an appointment card for the sonogram.

"You'll be feeling better in a few weeks. I promise," the nurse says.

I'm not so sure, Gabby thinks as she looks down at the rectangular scrap of paper. This cannot be happening. She wills her fingers to stop shaking.

Gabby sits in her car. *What do I do now?* She picks up her phone and scrolls through her contacts. She wants to tell someone; she needs to tell someone or she will go crazy. This news is tearing her apart—piece by piece her insides are ripping away. Her dreams of the future are crashing down like an implosion of a building wired for demolition. Will she survive? Gabby starts to dial Rita's number but stops, remembering that Rita and her dad are still on their honeymoon. She can't burden them. Lord knows she can't tell Brett. She needs to figure this out. *Take some deep breaths.*

There is Ella, but Ella is terrible at keeping a secret. She closes her eyes and sighs. No, she can't tell anyone.

She is going to be sick again. She opens her car door, leans over, and retches. The tears roll down her cheeks, and round moist spots glare up at her from the asphalt. What is she to do? She's alone and lost. One terrible night when she didn't use her voice is now threatening to destroy her future. Her sobs are uncontrollable.

CHAPTER 5

Gabby

After washing her face, Gabby stares in the mirror. Her hair is a mess but is second to the large, dark circles under her eyes. Are these circles an outward sign of the raging inner battle or just a symptom of the morning sickness? She remembers the words of the doctor. "It will pass in a few weeks. You'll feel much better in your second trimester." She never got the prescription filled. It's as if she is paying penance for getting herself in this state. She thought she was smarter. She applies her makeup concealer in an attempt to hide the dark circles.

She is managing Art Smart during Rita's absence. She is glad the first hour after opening the gallery is slow, as business increases closer to mid-morning. Once more, Gabby picks up the phone and dials the clinic in Houston. Time is her enemy. After several unsuccessful calls earlier today, this time, she stays on the line. Her heart is racing, and her stomach is churning.

"How may I direct your call?" the voice on the other end asks.

"I'd like information concerning an abortion."

"Is your pregnancy confirmed by a medical professional?"

"Yes."

"How many weeks?"

"Ten, well, maybe eleven," Gabby answers in a shaky voice.

The woman on the phone gives advice. "It is best to perform abortions in the first trimester. Can you get here next week? I have an opening on Tuesday. Of course, you will need to schedule a consultation on Monday. It's required."

Gabby is silent. She takes a deep breath, and she tries to control her jittery nerves.

"Sound good? You will be twelve weeks." Gabby thinks the woman's tone is condescending.

"Can I call you back?" Gabby manages to ask.

"Ma'am, I can't hold appointments. You will need to call me back as soon as possible. Have a nice day." The line is disconnected.

Gabby repeats in disbelief what the woman said, "Have a nice day." *What planet is that woman from? Yes, I'm having a nice day as I try to schedule an appointment to kill my baby. Do murderers have the right to have a nice day?* She wrings her hands.

Having an abortion will fix her problem. She will slip away for a few days; tell everyone that she's attending an art seminar in Houston, take some of her paintings, and use the opportunity to visit a few galleries. No one will be the wiser. Brett will never find out. Richard will never know. Her daddy will never know.

There is a sharp pain in her stomach when she thinks about how her daddy would react if he ever found out about the abortion. King is a proud Texan with great integrity, who speaks with God every day.

She knew that he would tremble knowing the sin she is contemplating. She reaches for her trinity knot necklace and slides the knot back and forth on the chain. "Mother, I need you. What should I do?"

Oh, it would be so nice to share her dilemma with a friend. However, there is no one she can trust. She sighs again as her shoulders slump, as if the burden she carries is so heavy she cannot stand upright.

Rita and her dad are still away on their honeymoon, visiting Rita's family on the East Coast. Will Rita be upset if she finds out that Gabby closed the gallery to go to Houston? Working at the gallery has provided Gabby with a convenient excuse to stay off the tennis courts and away from her friends. She has been able to hide her bouts of morning sickness. *Here I go again.* She darts into the bathroom.

While in the bathroom, she hears the bells on the door jingle, alerting her that a client has come into the store.

"Hey, Gabby, you here?" a familiar voice calls out.

God, it's Ella. Gabby straightens her hair and skirt and yells, "I'll be there in a second." After taking a few deep breaths and refreshing her lipstick, she pinches her cheeks in hopes of disguising her pale face. Stepping out of the bathroom, she sees Ella viewing some of the new ceramic pieces that recently arrived.

Gabby fakes a smile. "Hello, Ella. It's so nice to see you. What's new?" From Ella's dress, Gabby knows that she just came from playing tennis.

Ella turns to hug her, and Ella's mouth drops open. "Oh my God! You look awful."

Gabby isn't surprised and tries to make light of Ella's remark. "I have been under the weather."

"Are you contagious? You've seen a doctor, right?" Ella asks as she backs away to put a safe distance between them.

Gabby also steps back. "Yes, I've seen a doctor and no, I'm not contagious." *Oops, that was a mistake.* Why didn't she say she had the flu?

Ella wrinkles her brow as she looks more closely. "So, what's wrong?" However, without waiting for a reply, she flops down on the couch, flips off her shoes, and starts thumbing through one of the magazines. Gabby is relieved that she is no longer under scrutiny.

She knows that her best friend is settling in for a girl-to-girl chat. But at least the topic of her illness has passed. *I wonder what pressing news has brought Ella to search for me at the gallery.* Ella's eyes are bright and Gabby feels her positive energy. Something big is happening. Ella's joyfulness dampens Gabby's spirits even more. She wishes she could confide in Ella as easily as her friend can confide in her.

"Your dad's wedding was Fab-U-Lous!" Ella says, "And Rita's sons...smart, nice, and handsome. I can't believe that neither is attached. Really, what's wrong with those gals in D.C.?" She continues to turn the pages of the magazine but clearly isn't interested in any of the photos or articles. "Will calls me every day."

Okay, now we're finally getting down to the reason for this visit, Gabby thinks.

"Really?" Gabby soaks in Ella's glowing happiness.

"Yes, really!" Ella giggles. "He's flying here this weekend just to see me. He wants us to get to know one another better." She looks up from the magazine. "He's renting a condo in Galveston at the beach. Tax season will be over so he can take some vacation time."

"I thought you had to work on weekends," Gabby sits on the other end of the couch.

"I'm not missing this. I'll tell my boss there was an emergency in the family. Or I'm sick. I'll make up some excuse." Ella sees Gabby staring out the window. "Gabby, are you listening? This is my news flash of the year. Isn't it great?"

Gabby rubs her chin. "Be careful, Ella. Take your time and slow down."

Ella sticks out her lower lip. "Why can't you be happy for me?"

"I am happy for you, Ella. I want my best friend to be happy. In the past, you've gone full speed, and when the relationship is over, you're devastated. Do I need to remind you that you and Will just met?"

Ella quips, "Okay, Mother. I know that your love life is close to perfect. Everyone isn't as lucky."

Gabby sets her shoulders back, but hesitates and decides not to respond. *If Ella only knew that her perceived view of my life is so wrong.*

"Speaking of your love, I saw Brett at the club. Hot as ever, that one." Ella puts the magazine down. "When is Rita coming back? I miss my doubles partner. The league starts next week. We need to practice. You need to practice, girlfriend." She points her finger at Gabby. "We want an undefeated season, right? Once again the Gabby-Ella duo will rock." She gets up from the couch and moves her arms as if hitting an imaginary forearm stroke.

Gabby is still staring out the window. Ella says, "Earth to Gabby. Earth to Gabby."

"I'm so sorry. I have a lot on my mind. I haven't been sleeping well lately. I've been at the gallery every day now for two weeks.

This makes me grateful that I don't have to work full-time to support myself—even though compared to most jobs, this one is pretty easy."

Ella sits back down on the couch, and Gabby says, "I miss playing tennis. And I miss all of my friends." She gives Ella's shoulders a hug. "Sorry, partner, if you feel I let you down. I'll get Brett to hit with me this evening. Okay?" She looks for signs of forgiveness as she searches Ella's face.

"When are you moving in with Brett?" Ella asks. "Or is he moving in with you?"

"What?" Gabby gasps. "Brett told you?"

"Yeah, he told me. I thought I would hear something like that from you, not him. You, girlfriend, are the buzz of the club."

Gabby leans forward and stares at Ella.

"Don't act so surprised. Nobody at the club can believe it. Brett, the club playboy, is off the market. It's headline news." She pushes her shoulder into Gabby. "You're one lucky gal," she teases.

Gabby shakes her head. "I can always count on you to keep me up to date on the latest gossip around the club."

Ella ignores the remark. "Gabby, do you have time to go shopping? I need to buy a sexy negligee for Will. I want to give that boy a real Texas welcome."

Gabby is relieved that Ella hasn't pressed her for an answer about Brett. She responds quickly to the change in topic. "Sure, if you can wait a few days until Rita and Daddy are back."

"I'll wait." Ella stands up and stretches. "It's so awesome—Rita and your dad—so romantic. Think about it, Gabby. Your mother dies, and it's the end of the world for your dad. Then, there's a spark of love that ignites into a roaring flame and then, *bam*...romance, a chance to love again, sealed with forever vows." She lifts her arms as if in flight and dances around the gallery. "At sixty, you're off on a honeymoon. Come on, Gabby, smile. Your dad and Rita are living the dream that we all wish for." She finishes her dance and returns to the couch. "Pretty awesome, starting life over again."

For the sake of her mother, Gabby feels the need to correct Ella. "It's not starting life over. It's called moving forward." She reaches for the chain around her neck.

Ella looks down. "You know what I meant." She takes Gabby's hands. "Hey, what's going on with you? You don't sound very happy for them."

"I am happy for them," Gabby argues.

"I hardly recognize my girl. Usually, you're always so positive. Are you and Brett fighting?"

"No, no, it's nothing like that. I told you I've been sick, and I'm tired."

"You do look terrible. Guess I told you that already. So...what's wrong with you?"

"Something I ate—food poisoning," she lies. "It will pass in due time."

"Okay, okay. Let's plan to go shopping on Friday after tennis. We'll have a girls' shopping day. We are way overdue. I need to look my best for Will, and you can get something nice for Brett!" Ella gets up and opens the door. She calls back over her shoulder, "I hope you feel better soon."

"Thanks, me too."

After the door closes she gives a big sigh and wipes her brow. Thank God Ella's gone. She doesn't wish to hold the truth from her best friend, but until she makes a decision about her dilemma, she'll have to be careful about how much information she reveals.

That afternoon, Gabby paints as she has done every afternoon at the gallery. In the past, she has found her voice through her painting, and she has hopes that the canvas in front of her will begin a conversation. Over the weeks that she has been overseeing the gallery, she has painted several abstract paintings, but none of them have given her any answers to her current dilemma.

Today she focuses on the canvases that she previously prepared with the penciled design of the zeppelin bend knot. The single full-front view of this knot was the subject of the painting she had gifted her daddy and Rita for their wedding, but her work today depicts that same knot spread over two canvases making a diptych—each canvas a mirror image of the other as the knot is symmetrical. Praying that her creative voice is found, she starts to outline the image of the knot with dark purple paint. Then she paints one strand of the rope gold and the other, silver. Her brush follows the rope as it twists and turns, forming the knot. When she finishes with the brushwork, she separates the canvases. Each canvas contains the end of a rope in one of the colors and two loops.

She stands back to view her work. She blinks her eyes and cocks her head to the side. The canvas has given her an answer. Now the solution to her problem is obvious. Each single canvas has a strong composition and can stand by itself. She will not be calling the abortion agency back. She will not be going to Houston. She has a plan. Standing back with her hands on her hips she critiques the canvas again, searching for a flaw in her craftsmanship. She finds none.

The relief that sweeps over her causes her to take a sole canvas in her arms as she lowers her body to the floor. She lies on her back and holds the painting above her at arm's length. This is her answer. She had divided the zeppelin bend weeks ago, dividing it perfectly into two halves. One half is a painting in its own right. Just as the single rope with the two loops can stand alone, she and her baby can stand alone. She reaches her hand up in the air and gives thanks to God. She also asks for his protection and guidance in the journey she is about to embark upon. Her stomach rumbles, and for the first time in weeks, she is hungry.

She is a King, and she was raised a Christian. She will have this baby. She will decide later whether she will raise the baby as a single mom or if she will put it up for adoption. She will go away for a few months, have the baby and then return. She has plenty of time to figure everything out. Will Brett be supportive? Will he leave her? She frowns as she wishes a future with him. Is it too much to think he will understand? Why couldn't he be the father? It all would be so simple. He wanted to take their relationship to the next level. They would just be on the fast track. But with the pregnancy now at eleven weeks, the baby's father is not Brett; it is Richard. She shudders. It will be best not to tell Richard or Brett.

Gabby doesn't have all the answers, but one thing she does know; she knows she cannot go through with an abortion. It would haunt her. The price is too high for a quick, easy fix. Having the baby will be an inconvenience but nothing she can't learn to deal with. However, can she learn to deal with a life without Brett? He said that he loved her. Could he still love her knowing she is carrying another man's baby?

CHAPTER 6

Gabby

G abby, you haven't touched your dinner," says Brett. "We can order something else." He takes her hand. He met her at Art Smart, and they walked to the small restaurant on the other side of the shopping center.

"The food is fine. I'm just not hungry." She pushes the food around on the plate with her fork.

"You haven't been yourself now for weeks," he says. "I can trace this mood back to when I asked you to move in together." He shakes his head. "You seemed happy with the idea at first. What happened?"

Gabby wants to tell him. Every cell in her heart wants to tell him. What is stopping her? It is the fear of his reaction. She doesn't want to chance that he will get up, walk away, and their relationship will be over. It is too much for her to bear. How does one tell the person she loves that she is carrying another man's child? She swallows hard and doesn't use her voice.

"Your silence speaks volumes," Brett says. "It's obvious that you don't think it's a good idea." His face is drawn in despair.

He looks down and, sensing his disappointment, she reaches across the table for his hand, but he pulls it away.

"Okay, that's my answer. If it's that hard for you to discuss, then clearly, it isn't the right thing to do."

She knows that he deserves an explanation.

"If not now, then maybe not ever." He pushes his chair away from the table. "I can't do this anymore." He turns around and is gone.

Stunned, she looks around the restaurant. She wants more time. She needs more time, but she must follow him and explain. She tries to stand; however, her rapid heartbeat prevents her from moving. The pounding in her ears is loud, and her legs feel as if they are encased in cement. She feels dizzy. Is she going to faint? In a minute her dizziness passes, and she runs to the front door. "Brett, Brett, let me explain. Brett!"

His car is pulling out of the parking lot, the convertible top down and the music blaring. The tires screech. He is gone. She places her hands on her thighs, inhales deeply, and starts to sob.

Gabby walks across the parking lot back to Art Smart, struggling to catch her breath. Brett was so angry. Why couldn't she tell him about the baby? She opens the door to the gallery and is careful to find her way to the back room without turning on the lights. She doesn't want shoppers to think that the studio is open. She sits on the couch and closes her eyes. It is best to let him go. The baby is not his. Her heart is breaking and the tears flow.

An hour later, in the back of the gallery, she stands alone at her easel. After she mutes her cell and buries it deep in her purse, she turns on some classical music and addresses her canvas with brush in hand. She paints for strength. She paints for courage. She will paint the thoughts of her heart—thoughts about a love that she will sacrifice for her unborn child. Why does it hurt so much?

CHAPTER 7

Gabby

Gabby hears the beauty of the spring day in the song of the birds perched in the trees above the café's outdoor patio. However, the mood is not as cheerful between the best friends as Ella and Gabby eat their lunch. Breaking the awkward silence, Ella shakes her head.

"They weren't that good. How did we lose? I'm glad the rest of the team got the job done. But you and me, girlfriend…well, we played terribly."

"I'm sorry, Ella. It was my fault," Gabby says, putting her fork down and giving Ella her full attention. "I haven't been playing much lately with everything going on—my dad's wedding, managing the shop…" She takes a sip of her iced tea.

Ella says, "Not to mention Brett. When are the two of you going to make up?" She reaches for Gabby's arm. "It's so depressing to watch. He mopes around. You mope around. It's affecting your game, girl. My tennis partner is distracted. We lost today. Remember the Gabby-Ella

65

duo? We used to rock. Today was our first loss in two seasons." She folds her arms over her chest.

"I'm really sorry, okay?" Gabby looks down at the plate of salad in front of her.

"It's okay," Ella quips. "Really it is. I just wanted us to have one last win."

Gabby looks up and knits her brow.

"I guess now is as good a time as any to tell you," Ella says.

"Tell me what?"

"You need to find a new tennis partner."

Gabby's mouth drops open. "Over one loss, my best friend is dumping me?"

"It's not what you think. It has nothing to do with our loss today." Gabby can sense the urgency in Ella's voice. "I thought telling you after the match would be better than telling you before."

Gabby sits up straighter in her chair. She sees that Ella is glowing and that her sad attitude has vanished like a cloudy day graced by the sun's rays breaking through. "What's going on? Why are you smiling?"

"I have some amazing news. Well, at least I think it's pretty awesome." Ella takes a deep breath before continuing. "Remember I told you that I had a fabulous weekend in Galveston with Will? Well, it seems that he had a good time too," she adds as she shifts her weight and motions Gabby to lean in closer.

Ella whispers, "So good that Will asked me to move to D.C. Can you believe it?" Her eyes sparkle, and she gives a small squeal.

"He did what?" Gabby stares wide-eyed and gasps. "What did you tell him?"

Ella sits back in her chair and pushes a brown curl behind her ear.

"Well, I said yes of course." She crosses her arms, with a huge smile. She winks. "I guess that negligee did the trick!"

Gabby is stunned. "That's kind of fast, don't you think? You hardly know each other."

Ella rubs her chin. "You're right, we don't know each other well, but we can have fun learning about each other as we go along. I wasn't going to take the risk of Will changing his mind. I really like him, Gabby. I think he's the one." She adds, "If I don't move to D.C., I'll be sitting here in Texas, and I'll worry that he may find someone else."

"What about your job? Are you going to work until they find a replacement?"

"Well, that's where more good news comes in. This morning, I checked with our D.C. office. The receptionist there is going on maternity leave in a month. They were going to hire a temp to replace her, but I can take her position." She sits back in her chair. "The job is mine if I want it. It's perfect. It's like it was meant to be. I can move, take a month to learn my way around the city and spend time with Will before starting work. Perrr-fect!"

"What about your apartment?" Gabby asks, putting her fork down.

Ella says proudly, "I'm breaking the lease. Will said he would take care of everything. He's such a doll. I'll move my furniture to storage. If things go well in six months, I'll just call the thrift shop and donate everything."

Gabby shakes her head. "Wow! This is so fast."

"Gabby, be happy for me. No lectures, okay?" Ella looks at her sternly. "You seem to be having plenty of your own relationship problems. I don't think you are the one to be giving advice." She leans back and crosses her arms over her chest.

Gabby opens her mouth to speak but quickly closes it. Ella's remark stings, but she sucks in a breath and lets the remark slide. Ella is right. Her life really is a mess.

Ella flags down the waiter. "Two glasses of champagne, please."

Gabby starts to protest but stops. She sees the joy written all over Ella's face.

Ella says, "We need to toast to my new relationship. Please, please be happy for me. Promise me you'll come and visit."

"Of course, I'll visit. You're my best friend."

The waiter is quick to bring their champagne. Gabby sees the dancing effervescent bubbles and thinks the champagne mimics Ella's sparkle of enthusiasm for her new journey. *Ella makes life happen, for better or worse. Can I be as bold?* The crystal long-stemmed glass with its bubbly contents causes her to smile. *Oh, if life could be as lively— always dancing. Maybe my life is dancing too, just to a different rhythm.*

They clink their glasses together. "To new beginnings," Gabby says. After they sip, she looks at Ella with big eyes. "Come here, girl. I need to give you a hug. This is wonderful news. Good for you. I am very happy for you, girlfriend." Their embrace is warm and genuine.

"Thank you! It really means a lot to me. You mean a lot to me. You're like a sister to me. I love you. You know that, right?" Ella looks to Gabby as if she needs some reassurance.

Little does Ella know that Gabby will also have some new beginnings. She touches her stomach and wonders what her own future will hold. She takes a small sip of her champagne. The bubbles tickle her nose, and she smiles. She always wanted to be a mother. Some women never get the opportunity. It could be a wonderful experience. But her smile fades as she thinks of Brett. *I don't want to lose him. However, the baby must come first.*

Ella continues, "I'm sorry to be leaving you at the start of the season. Really I am." She touches Gabby's forearm. "Please don't be mad at me. I did you a favor, though."

Her thoughts interrupted, Gabby looks up from her plate. She has been pushing the green leaves around, hoping that Ella doesn't notice her lack of appetite. "You did me a favor?"

"Even though you and Brett are fighting, I asked him to find you a really nice partner. It's the least I can do since I'm abandoning you." Ella finishes her champagne. "There's this new gal. She moved here from Houston, and she seems really nice. And I hear she's a pretty good player. I think she would be perfect."

Gabby looks up with tears in her eyes. "I'll miss you, Ella. I know that you will be happy. Maybe Will is your Mr. Right." She takes her napkin and dabs her eyes. *Darn, I'm so emotional lately. It must be my hormones.* "When are you leaving?"

"I'm leaving Friday, right after work. I got my plane ticket this morning."

"Oh my, so soon!" She reaches over to hold Ella's hand.

"I know. I know. My parents are freaking out...but it feels right, Gabby. I know it won't be easy. I'll have to start over—meet new friends and struggle with a new job."

"Change is never easy, but it can be exciting," Gabby says, swirling her champagne around the glass, watching the bubbles. *Having a baby will be exciting and will certainly change my life.*

"If Will and I stay together, it will be worth it all, totally. And...if it doesn't, I won't be spending the rest of my life thinking about what if.

There will be no regrets, just growth." Gabby pinches her lips together. Ella sounds so mature.

"I want you to come and visit. Let me put it this way, I'll need you to come and visit." Ella reaches down for her purse and gets out her phone. "So, look at your calendar and give me a date. Right here, right now."

She slides her chair closer to Gabby. "I'm going to miss you so much. It will be easier for me, knowing that I will see you soon. Pick a date." She scrolls through her calendar to ensure that Gabby can see the screen.

"You need to come before I start work."

Gabby looks at the weeks ahead and shakes her head. *I have no idea what I will be doing in a few weeks. Just pick a date. Ella is not going to let this drop.* She randomly picks a weekend in the middle of the next month. "I'll need to clear this with Rita before it's definite,"

"We'll have such a good time," Ella assures her. "You didn't finish your champagne."

"You can have it," she says as she pushes the glass across the table. "I need to get to work." She checks her phone for the time as she stands and pushes back her chair.

Ella gulps down the last of the champagne. "I've got to get going too. I have so much to do before Friday."

Gabby watches as Ella skips to her car. She envies her friend's carefree, easy attitude. Ella seems really happy about moving to Washington. That gives Gabby an idea. Why hasn't she thought of this before?

Gabby opens the door to Art Smart and walks to the back to hang her jacket.

"Hello, Gabby! I'm so glad you're finally here," Rita yells. "I'm meeting your dad downtown. We have an appointment with the decorator from that new furniture store. The ranch house is looking a bit dreary and could use a facelift." She looks at her watch. "Oh dear, I need to hurry."

Gabby feels her stomach churn and a lump rise in her throat. *Change is difficult.* She is reminded of her advice to Ella just minutes before. Now, Rita is redecorating the ranch house. *Will she be getting rid of Anna's furniture?* Gabby bites her tongue and looks away. This is just one more thing that will push the memory of her mother further away. *I understand that you are gone, and now Rita is married to Daddy, but I won't forget you.*

"Thanks, Gabby," Rita calls as she opens the door to leave. "I'll take some photos of the furniture if we find anything we like. Bye." With a wave of her hand, she is gone.

That afternoon at the gallery, Gabby paints. Working at the gallery allows her this opportunity, and she has painted every afternoon since Rita hired her. When she paints, it allows her freedom of expression. And painting today will be much-needed therapy.

So much is going on inside her head—thoughts of Anna, thoughts of Ella and, more importantly, thoughts about the baby. Loading her palette, she squeezes some ultramarine blue from the tube and then pink madder. First, her brush dances in the blue paint: blue, the color of the sky; blue, the color of the water; blue, the color referring to a boy. She beams—a baby, a new life. Will her baby be a boy or a girl? In a few weeks, the sonogram will tell her, but does she wish to know? *What if*

I were to keep the baby? She touches her chin, in deep thought. Then she thinks of Brett. Would he accept Richard's child and raise him as his own? She has heard of men doing that. Who would be the wiser?

Continuing, she adds some pink paint to the canvas. *What if my baby is a girl?* This brings a quick smile. *I will name her Anna. Rita may get rid of Anna's furniture, but I will keep my mother's memory alive. Every time I use my little girl's name, I will think of my own sweet mother.*

"Anna—it has a nice ring to it," Gabby says aloud and gives a tiny giggle. With her brush loaded with rose madder paint, she purposefully touches the wet blue paint, creating a lush shade of lavender. It delights her, and she grins again. Girl or boy, it really doesn't matter. Either will be fine. How long has it been since she felt so carefree?

Continuing to have fun with the abstract painting, she squeezes out some yellow paint on her palate. Making a streak across the canvas, she gasps because she realizes that the green she created layering the yellow paint over the blue is the same hue as the green in Brett's eyes. Her hand goes to her mouth, and her carefree mood escapes. *Brett will never accept Richard's baby and raise it as his own. I need to call the adoption agency. I need to have a plan.*

She falls to her knees in an attempt to catch her heart as it has already sunk to her stomach. *I am silly to consider keeping a baby and raising it as a single mother.* She falls to the floor, grasping her trinity knot necklace. What is she to do?

CHAPTER 8

Gabby

Gabby stands on the curb and waits for King to join her. Looking into the clear sky, she soaks in the sun on this warm day in May. A week has passed since that afternoon at the gallery when her canvas gave an answer to her dilemma, and the most critical step in the execution of that plan begins today.

"Everything is arranged. Rita and I will visit you in a few weeks. You'll have plenty of time to think things through," King says. Gabby sees the tears in his eyes. The big, strong fearless Texan is really a big teddy bear.

"I love you, Daddy. I'll be fine, promise. I'll have a few months to figure it all out," she says as she looks down and unconsciously rubs her stomach.

"I love you too, Kitten. I'll miss you terribly. You know that, right?" He pulls her in for a hug. "Call me anytime—day or night, understand?"

"Thank you, Daddy." She can't stop the waterworks, and the tears spill down her cheeks. "Don't make me cry," she says as she wipes her face with her hand. "My makeup will run." She laughs.

"Have you spoken with Brett?" King asks as he rubs her back. Gabby shakes her head and looks away. "You're a grown woman, and I know you will make the right decision. Brett loves you, kitten. What do I tell him?" He turns his face away from her. "We'll be weaning the calves soon. Brett has already told Rusty that he will help. You know that he'll ask me. And ask me again. Please talk to him."

"I'm sorry if I am putting you in a bad position, but I need time to think. I don't know the answer so it's tough to tell him. When I figure it out, I'll let you know," She promises, crossing her chest. "Scout's honor."

He closes the trunk of the car and tips the porter who is about to haul her suitcase away.

"Give me one more hug, kitten. Call me when you land."

After they hug, she turns and steps through the airport doors. Saying goodbye is always a painful process, and she hadn't intended to linger. She chokes back her tears, sniffs, pulls back her shoulders, and takes a deep breath. *I can do this.*

The flight is three hours, and Gabby manages to grab an hour of much-needed rest. She is in her second trimester and is thankful the morning sickness is behind. She has even gained a few pounds. She smiles, recalling the support from Rita and her dad. Just telling them has lifted her spirits.

Thoughts of Brett cause her to look down at her watch. She clenches her jaw. Brett is probably giving a clinic. The ladies will be showering him with praise, and some will flirt with him. She frowns as Ella is no longer there to give a full report about the happenings around the club. How ironic. She used to roll her eyes as Ella shared the latest gossip. Now, she yearns for it.

Thinking about the gossip, she wonders what rumors members will spread after they realize that she is gone. She shakes her head. She tried calling Brett twice in the past day, but he didn't respond. She even left a voice mail message. Really, she was relieved that he didn't pick up. It was much easier leaving a message telling him that she would be out of town than actually talking to him.

She touches her stomach. The hot summer months in Texas will not allow her to hide her pregnancy any longer. She doesn't fit into her tennis clothes and knows she will be much more comfortable wearing maternity clothing. It's best for her to leave. She has told herself this for weeks, but she knows her daddy is right. She really should be open and honest with Brett. Will he miss her? Will he contact her? She closes her eyes and stares out the window at the clouds in the sky. They look so fluffy and carefree. She sinks lower in her seat and swings the knot on her chain back and forth.

Brett

Later that same day after work, Brett has returned to his apartment, and he is angry. He replays the voice message over and over as he paces back and forth. *God, that woman is so frustrating.* He pushes the button on his answering machine once again as he tries to read between the lines of her message.

"Brett, this is Gabby. I know you're angry with me. This is hard... but I realize that I owe you an explanation. Umm... I'm leaving town for a while. I don't expect you to understand." She pauses. He hears her take a deep breath. "I'm so sorry..." There is another longer pause and then a click telling him the line is disconnected.

He frowns. From the tone of Gabby's voice and her fragmented sentences, he is sure something is wrong. She has been acting strange and aloof for weeks. It started before their fight at the restaurant. *Is she sick?* He knits his brow. He's thought of going over to the gallery many times, but he was so hurt. She didn't want to live together, and he was hoping that she would miss him so much that when he put distance between them, she would come begging. He purposely didn't text or phone her. It was a test. He needed her to prove her love. This was not the outcome he anticipated. He puts the phone on the coffee table.

He hangs his head and whispers, "Gabby, what are you doing? You're destroying us."

Brett reaches for the whiskey bottle sitting on his coffee table and pours a glass. He was so sure she would come back, and his pride kept him from reaching out to her. He misses her and wants her so much that it scares him. He stares at the trinity knot painting that he bought at her art reception earlier this year. He recalls her joy the first time she came to his apartment and saw it on the mantle. But now she's gone, and he shakes his head as he lifts the glass to his lips. Was she that upset with him that she had to leave town to avoid running into him? He hasn't seen her at the tennis club lately. He can't even use Ella as a sounding board. She's gone too.

He knows that Gabby is cautious and tries to look at a situation from all angles before making a decision. Now, he curses under his breath, feeling foolish that he didn't march over to the gallery or her apartment and demand that she speak to him. He knows that if he had gotten her in his arms, she would have caved, and he could convince her to tell him everything. They would have talked, and this whole mess would be in the past—something they could laugh about over dinner and drinks in the future. Did they even have a future? He knows what they shared was special. Didn't she feel it? Is it too late now?

PART II

CHAPTER 9

Gabby

After stopping at the restroom to freshen her makeup and brush her hair, Gabby makes the long hike to baggage claim. She wants to look her best.

Standing at the carousel, she hears his familiar voice, and she turns around.

"There you are. I have been looking all over for you." Stan grins. "I thought you missed your flight. I'm so glad you're here." He gives her a big hug.

She looks up into his kind, earnest face. His smile is contagious, causing her to smile back.

"Wow, you look fabulous," Stan says, standing back and looking at her at arm's length. "I'm so excited. I have thought of nothing else since Mother called me. How was your flight?"

"It was great." Is that happy voice her own? She reaches down to pull her suitcase off the carousel, but he stops her. "You shouldn't be lifting in your condition." He grabs her bag and places it beside them.

She blushes and avoids looking at him.

"How many bags do you have?"

Gabby looks at the carousel. "All the bags that are left," she says, pointing to the last two large bags making their round again.

"Those big ones?" He smiles and she knows that he is teasing.

"A girl needs a proper wardrobe. It's not like I'm staying for a week, you know. I guess most of these clothes won't even fit in another week or two. What was I thinking?"

"We have some great stores here. We can go shopping. It'll be fun." He stacks her bags on a cart and starts wheeling out to the sidewalk. She follows him. He seems so confident and in control. *Yes, Stan will take good care of me. Coming here was the right decision.*

"I made us a dinner reservation. I thought you would be hungry. Sound good?" He pauses briefly. "Le Chateau, it's French. Is that all right? We can change if you would like something else."

"No, that's fine. I love French food." She nods as their cab comes to the curb.

"It's one of my favorites. I think you'll like it too," he says proudly as he takes a seat in the back of the taxi next to her.

"Am I dressed okay? It sounds fancy."

"My dear, you look great. You'll be the most beautiful woman there. No one will even question your clothing."

"Thank you." She pushes her hand against her stomach.

She takes his hand and looks into his deep brown eyes. "I really need a friend right now. Thanks for allowing me to hang out with you." She gives his hand a squeeze. "I hope it won't be too much of an imposition." His hand is warm and firm, making her feel confident that she has made a wise decision in coming here.

He, in return, pats her hand. "Nonsense, you can't possibly be any trouble. I love having guests. We'll be good for each other. Mother gave me the abridged version, but you can fill me in on the rest. Well, that's if you want to tell me. I don't mean to pry." This time, he squeezes her hand. "I want to help. Talking things through always works for me." She smiles. Stan has a good soul. It was wise to ask Rita to help her make a plan.

Stan's condo is on the eleventh floor and has a view of downtown Washington. Compared to Brett's bachelor pad, Stan's place is lavish. He lives in a two-bedroom high-rise, just across the Potomac River, and only one block from the Metro line. Everything in the condo is coordinated, from the drapes and furniture to the rugs on the floor. Nothing is out of place. She wonders if he hired a decorator.

After Stan shows her to her room, she unpacks her suitcases. She empties the bag that has a few of her maternity clothes and hangs them in the spacious closet. She hopes she won't have to wear them for another week or two. However, she can feel she's expanding. Why did she bring all of these clothes? She is thankful that Stan didn't ask her any questions during their dinner earlier. Her insides are sore from all of the laughter. She appreciates his dry sense of humor. Laughing is better for her than any medicine. Her mood is much lighter, and she feels grateful.

The bedroom where she will be staying is painted in a cheery yellow, and the dark cherry furniture gives the room a rich, traditional look.

Thirty minutes later, there's a knock at the door.

"Yes," she answers. "Come in."

"How is everything?" He steps inside. "Do you like your room?" Not waiting for her answer he says, "We can take the artwork off the walls so you can hang your own. It will make it seem more like home, don't you think?"

"Everything is perfect. The flowers are a nice touch." Gabby points to the vase of daisies on the dresser. "And the slippers and the robe. I didn't bring any artwork with me. You really didn't need to do all of this."

"Yes, I did." He was beaming. "You have so many wildflowers growing in Texas I thought they might make you feel more at home. I'm glad you like them. It makes me happy to see you happy. Can I make a suggestion?"

"Of course," She tilts her head to one side.

"Take a nice, long bath. I put some bubble bath on the counter. You must be exhausted." He motions toward the bathroom door.

"Perfect, that would be really nice. I am tired."

"If you need anything, let me know."

"I can't think of anything. You really have thought of everything. Thank you, again." She looks up at him and smiles.

"You're welcome. Sleep well." He winks before closing the door.

The next morning, Gabby awakens to the smell of coffee. She goes to the window and opens the drapes. It was too dark after returning from dinner to get the full scope of the view. Looking out, she sees the Washington Monument towering a few miles away. She isn't sure about many things these days, but she is very certain that she's not in Texas anymore.

Donning the soft robe that Stan placed in the closet, she makes her way to the kitchen. Stan looks up from his iPad. "Hello, angel, how did you sleep?"

"Well, thank you. I was really tired." She sees him staring at her and runs her hands through her hair. "I must look a mess."

His eyes shift back down at the table. "A gorgeous mess," he whispers.

She can feel the heat rising in her cheeks.

"Here, have some coffee." He pours coffee from his carafe into the cup at the second place setting on the small breakfast room table. "I'm leaving you alone today because I need to work. Sorry, I took yesterday off, and my boss won't give me a second day. Spring is our busiest time of the year. However, I have a few minutes before I need to leave." He pushes his chair back from the table a bit and gestures for her to take a seat. "So…talk to me, Gabby. Anything you tell me is confidential. I promise."

She plays with the spoon, swirling the coffee round and round in the mug, trying to put the right words together.

He starts their conversation. "So, you're pregnant. You're almost twenty-nine. Why can't I say congratulations? Why are you hiding?"

She remains quiet and continues to stir her coffee.

"Let me make a guess—Brett isn't ready to be a father." Stan reaches over and takes her hand.

"Brett doesn't know," she says quietly as she turns away, not wanting to see his reaction.

He chokes on his coffee. "What? You didn't tell him?" He shakes his head. "I'm your friend, you know that right? But Brett has rights as the baby's father."

She bites her lip before she gains the courage to face him. Staring back is a kind, understanding face. "Brett's not the father." There, she's said those painful words.

Stan's eyes are wide. "What?" He realizes that he has raised his voice. "Oh, sorry, I'm not judging. I'm just surprised, that's all."

"It's not what you think." She twists her fingers together.

"Like I said I'm not judging. I got the impression when I was in Texas for Mother's wedding that you and Brett were really tight." He makes a gesture crossing his two fingers.

Still feeling the heat that has risen in her face, she explains, "We are tight. We're great together. Everything was so perfect..."

"So...how did this happen?"

"I got pregnant before Brett and I started dating. If the doctor's calculations are correct, I must have been about two weeks along before Brett."

"Do you know who the father is?"

She feels awkward discussing something so personal. However, he has opened his home to her, and she does need a friend.

"I got pregnant in January when I was with a guy named Richard. We had dated for a few years but then the relationship fell apart, and he moved out shortly thereafter." She can finally look at him again.

"Is your doctor sure of the date?"

"I haven't had a paternity test, but I'm too far along for the baby to be Brett's."

He scratches his chin. "Have you told this guy, what's his name...Richard?"

"No, of course not."

"And why not?"

She realizes that Stan is asking very legitimate questions, and she does owe him some kind of explanation. "Because he's not a very nice person." She takes a sip of her coffee.

"You must not have always thought that."

Her shoulders slump. "At first, Richard was wonderful. It was fun and exciting and yes, I thought I loved him. But then..." She turns away and swallows hard. "Then he lied, and he was cheating on me. I haven't told him I'm pregnant since I really don't want him in my life. And the first week or two after finding out, I considered having an abortion. There would be no need to tell him anything. But I couldn't go through with it."

She takes a sip of her coffee before continuing. "Richard's running for the Senate. I don't want some ambitious reporter snooping around. I don't want to be part of a scandal that is smeared across the news. Let's see, how would that headline read—Candidate Running for Senate Has Illegitimate Child? I thought it best to get out of Texas."

"What do you think he'll do when he finds out?"

"Richard?" She shifts her weight in the chair. "If he knew, he would want us to get married. You see, from the beginning, Daddy and Richard had a plan. First, Richard would run for senator and then after a few years, they'd rally enough support to take him to the governor's mansion. My daddy thought I would look great standing next to Richard as he advanced his political career." She plays with her napkin and bites her lip.

"Daddy told me, 'Texas will love you, trust me.' I can see it clearly. Richard will use me, his pregnant wife, and later the baby to pull at

87

the heartstrings of the public so they'll vote for him. We will appear to be the perfect, happy family."

"From your sarcastic tone, you don't want that scenario so—what do you want?"

"I could never marry Richard. As I told you, I ruled out having an abortion. However, do I keep the baby or give it up for adoption? I keep changing my mind." She pauses as if thinking aloud. "An abortion would have been such an easy fix: one afternoon away, then a few days of rest, and then Brett and I would continue on. It would have been so simple and perfect."

"But you didn't have the abortion."

"No." She sighs. "I couldn't do it. I can't take an innocent life. How can I live my life knowing that I killed my baby?" She searches Stan's face for approval. He takes a sip of coffee and then leans back in the chair.

He remains matter-of-fact. "I see. So what is your plan?"

"Have the baby, then either give it up for adoption or keep it. And I lose Brett." Her voice trails off.

Stan's eyes light up and he seems surprised. "Whoa! How did you make that giant leap?"

She pauses and turns her head toward the wall. "Brett won't understand. I can't expect him to raise another man's child."

"How do you know that?" Stan asks. "Don't you think he should be making that decision?"

"Why would he want to raise another man's child?" She turns to face him. "You're a single guy. What would you do if you were in Brett's shoes?"

Stan takes her hands in his own once more. "Gabby, look at me,

I know you're emotional. It's a big decision, and your hormones are off the chart, but listen to me, any guy would be crazy to give up on you." He searches her eyes. "Are you hearing me? The pregnancy was an accident. It happened before you and Brett were together. Life happens. You learn to roll with the punches." He squeezes her hands tight. "Take a few days, a few weeks. Think it over."

She hangs her head and he says, "I'm going to leave you with one more thought. Well, really it's a quote: 'Love conquers all.' I think you are underestimating the power of love."

He checks his watch. "With those words of wisdom, I need to get to work. If you need anything—phone, text, whatever, and I'll get back to you ASAP. Everything will work out, you'll see."

He stands and grabs the black leather jacket from the back of the chair. He picks up his gloves and his helmet. She stares.

"This is me, Gabby—the motorcycle guy, the mechanic," he says as he puts on his jacket and zips up.

"I'm sorry if I was staring. I've just never seen you dressed like this. It's such a different look from the guy who let a horse throw him." She giggles. "It's a good look. You wear it well."

"Thank you," he says, beaming. "I'll be home around six. We can have dinner here or go out. Your call." He flips his keys in the air. "There're some books on the shelf, and I have a surprise for you in the laundry room closet." He opens the front door to leave. "Something to keep you busy. Bye." He waves before the door closes behind him. His cheery whistle fades, farther and farther away until he is gone.

Gabby finishes her coffee and eats a muffin from the package on the table. It is a blueberry muffin with lots of sugar crystals on top. *Yumm. Does Stan always partake in something so sinful or did he splurge on my account?* Being pregnant has allowed her to stray from her usual, healthy, calorie-conscientious meals. *Ah, the benefits of pregnancy.* She grins as she pours some orange juice. She feels better after the difficult conversation with Stan. It does help to talk with others.

Her curiosity is getting the best of her. *What surprise is waiting for me in the closet?* She makes her way to the laundry room and opens the closet door. A large cardboard box sits front and center with an envelope, her name scrawled on it. She rips it open. There is just a single word in large, bold print staring at her: ENJOY. What could it be?

Gabby slides the box out into the foyer and opens the flaps. She removes the bags one by one. The first bag has a variety of brushes and palette knives. The second has tubes of acrylic paints. The remainder of the contents of the box has canvases of different sizes and a palette. Taped to the palette is another message. "Look on the balcony." With haste, she runs to the small porch. Propped in the corner behind a plant is an easel. *He thinks of everything. My first painting is going to be the perfect painting for this condo.*

Immediately, she gets her phone and sends a text to Stan: "Thank you, thank you. I think your bachelor pad needs a masterpiece!" On her phone appears a missed call from Ella. Gabby rolls her eyes and shakes her head. Yes, Ella. She will need to share her news; there is no way to avoid it any longer. With hesitation, she pushes Call Back.

"Hi, Ella!" Gabby takes in a deep breath. "I saw your missed call. How is D.C.?"

"D.C. is good. Hey, hold on a second, Gabby."

A minute later Ella is back on the line. "Sorry, I had to finish another call. I'm at work, but I can talk. It's good to hear from you."

"How's the new job?" Gabby asks.

"Gabby, the job is great. I'm enjoying it. I didn't think I would like the city, but it's growing on me."

"How's it going with Will?"

"Will is so wonderful. I pinch myself every day to be sure I'm not dreaming. Right now, everything is pretty awesome." Ella giggles. "I hated leaving Texas, but D.C. has so much to see and to do. I'm having a ball with the man of my dreams." There is a slight pause. "I miss you, girlfriend. You're coming to visit, right? It's on my calendar, and you promised."

"Actually, Ella, I'm here, right now. I just got in late last night."

Ella squeals, and Gabby holds the phone away from her ear.

"That's great. When can I see you? I'm pretty open—lunch, dinner, you name it."

"Lunch? Today?"

"Seriously? Wow, fantastic. This is a wonderful surprise. There's this great little Italian restaurant near here called Romeo's. It's at Fourteenth and G Street. One p.m.?"

"I'll find it," Gabby says.

"I'm so excited. I can't wait to see you."

"Me too. See you at one." *I guess today is as good a day as any to tell Ella.*

She looks at the paints and the brushes, disappointed that she will have to use them another day. She sighs as she places them back in the box and returns the box to the closet. She needs to see Ella and explain, because she doesn't wish Stan to avoid his brother or lie to Will in order to keep her secret. It is not her intent to cause Stan any hardships. It will be good to get this matter out of the way, and the sooner the better.

CHAPTER 10

Gabby

Gabby knows her way around Washington with its Metro system as she was here for an art conference a few years ago. It's a more modern system than the New York City subway. She easily transfers to the Red Line and has only one stop until she exits for a three-block walk to Romeo's. Flowers are growing in planters along the street. She smiles as they are just budding on this cool, comfortable day in May. In Texas, these same flowers have already been in full bloom for a few weeks. She stops on the sidewalk to text Stan because she doesn't want him to worry if he calls the home phone and she doesn't answer.

Across the street, a bright red awning with white letters alerts her that she has arrived at her destination. She gets a booth and orders some iced tea. She mentally rehearses her speech because she wants this girl-to-girl talk to go smoothly, and she needs to trust that Ella will keep her secret.

"Hey, you!" Ella says as she comes in the front door and sees Gabby sitting in the booth. She holds both of her arms out for a hug.

"Hey, yourself. You look fabulous. Is that a new outfit?" Gabby asks as they hug.

Ella takes a seat. "It sure is. Thanks for noticing. They dress a little more conservative here. I really want to fit in, so I had to buy a few new pieces for my wardrobe."

"Love must agree with you. You sound great."

"Thank you! Will is awesome. Who would have thought that I would be living here with my soul mate? We're so happy. But enough about me—I've missed you. How long will you be in town?"

"That's what I need to talk to you about," Gabby says.

"If you need a place to stay, you can stay with us."

"No, no, nothing like that. I have something important to share with you. You can share with Will but no one else. Understand?"

Ella takes a sip of her tea. "You're being rather mysterious."

"Ella, promise me. Mum's the word, okay?"

"God, I promise." She throws her arms up in the air, then brings them down and crosses her fingers, adding, "Hope to die."

The waiter comes and takes their order. Gabby places her elbows on the table and leans forward. "I'm going to be here a few months."

"You're staying for the entire exhibition?"

"There is no exhibition," she says, looking intensely at Ella. "Well, at least, not yet."

"Why are you here so long?"

"I needed to get out of Texas." Gabby brushes her hair back.

"But why? The heat never bothered you before."

94

"Ella, just shut up. I'm trying to tell you something. Please, can you listen? This is hard enough."

Ella touches her hand. "I'm sorry. I'm listening. You have my undivided attention." There is empathy in her voice.

"Okay, you ready for this?" Gabby takes a deep breath before continuing. "I'm pregnant."

"Wow, really? Congratulations!" Then Ella asks, "When are you and Brett getting married? You are getting married, right?" She cocks her head to the side and puts her finger to the side of her face as if in deep thought. "But wait, you said you were going to be here for a few months. Now, I'm really confused."

"It's complicated. Brett doesn't know."

Ella gasps. "The two of you still can't be fighting. Did you come here hoping he'd follow? That's romantic but ridiculous. That's not the behavior of the practical, level-headed girl I know."

"Ella, listen to me. Brett doesn't know, and I would like to keep it that way."

"I don't understand." Ella shakes her head. "Oh...you're going to get an abortion."

"No. I can't bring myself to do that. I'm going to have the baby."

"When are you due?"

"The end of October."

Ella starts counting backward. "You're almost four months, and you're just telling me? I'm supposed to be your best friend. Who keeps something like that from her best friend?"

"As I told you before, it's really complicated. It would be so easy if Brett were the father."

Ella's mouth drops open, but no sound comes forth.

"Richard is the father. It's his baby." She looks down, unable to face Ella.

The awkward silence is shortened by the perfect timing of the waiter bringing their salads. Gabby glances up and is faced with Ella's puzzled stare.

After the waiter leaves, Gabby says, "I decided to have the baby." She touches her stomach. "With Richard on the campaign trail for the Senate, I don't need a reporter getting news of this. And I certainly don't want Richard to know. Ella, you can tell Will but no one else. Understand?"

Ella stands. Gabby thinks she is going to the restroom, but instead, she reaches around and places her hand on Gabby's stomach. "Wow, you do have a little paunch. How cute!" This is not the reaction that Gabby expected.

"I'm about fifteen weeks," Gabby says in a matter-of-fact voice.

"This is so exciting." Ella beams.

She is surprised by Ella's enthusiasm.

"I said I was going to have the baby. However, I haven't decided if I am going to keep it or give it up for adoption." Gabby shifts her weight in her chair. "I need time to sort things out. I'm staying with Stan. He has been so supportive. He's been really kind."

Ella returns to her chair and quips, "Duh, of course he is kind and supportive."

"What do you mean by that?"

"Girl, you are so naïve. Don't tell me you haven't figured it out?"

Gabby's expression is blank, and she stares at Ella.

"You really don't know?"

"Know what, Ella?"

Ella wipes her mouth with the corner of her napkin before answering. "He likes you, or should I say loves you, silly. Will told me weeks ago. Not that Stan told Will, mind you. It's just the way Stan acts whenever we bring up your name."

"That's the silliest thing I've heard in a while. We just met at Daddy's wedding. Stan's my step-brother. His offer to help me—well, that's what families do. They take care of one another."

"Whatever, I'm just passing on to my best friend, the best friend who didn't tell me she was pregnant, that the guy who's there for her in her hour of need, loves her."

"That's just crazy. Who would want me in my condition?" With those words, Gabby is reminded of her conversation earlier this morning with Stan over coffee. She thought he was referring to Brett. Was he also including himself when he told her that love conquers all?

After lunch, Gabby follows Ella back to her office building.

"So this is where you work." She looks up at the old gray building.

"I know it doesn't look like much from the outside. But it's a great job, and I like my boss. I was glad to start work two weeks earlier than planned. The woman I was replacing had her baby early. It seems like babies don't adhere to a calendar and arrive in this world on their own schedule."

"I'll be finding that out soon enough," Gabby says with a giggle.

"I still can't believe you're pregnant." Ella puts her hands on her hips. "Hey, give me a hug, girlfriend. I need to get back to work." Gabby gives her a squeeze.

Ella says, "I'm really glad you came to D.C. Will and I don't have any plans for this weekend, so let's go out to dinner. Find out if Stan is free." She waves as she turns and goes through the door. "I'll call you." Ella blows a kiss.

Gabby walks a few blocks and takes in the noise, smells, and sights of the city. *No, I'm not in Texas anymore.* This bustling place is going to be her home for at least the next five months. She descends the steps to the Metro. She's happy that Ella seems to have made the right decision in moving here. Ella changed her life—new city, new job, and a new man. Can she do the same? She grins as she recalls Ella's words referring to Stan, "Duh, he loves you, silly."

CHAPTER 11

Gabby

Days seem to go by quickly. It has been a busy week as Gabby explores her new surroundings. She finds a doctor to continue her prenatal care. She researches art galleries in hopes of finding a fit for her artwork. Living with Stan is easy, but she misses her friends and family in Texas. Having Ella living close has been a godsend. She has been very supportive and almost motherly in a sense, which is totally opposite from the Ella that Gabby has known since college. It seems that Ella is happy and more stable now that she is in a serious relationship.

As she unlocks the condo door, her cell phone rings.

"Hi, honey. How is life in Washington?"

"Fine, Daddy. I'm getting to know my way around, but I'm not much for living in the city. I guess it will just take time, although Ella loves it here, and I'm happy for her."

"I can relate. I'm not much of a city-dweller either. You must take after your old man. How about you, kitten? How are you and the baby?"

She wishes he wouldn't use the word *baby*. She is trying her best to keep a distance between herself and the bump growing inside.

"With the morning sickness stopped, being pregnant is a bit more tolerable. I get tired easily." She gives a yawn, takes off her shoes, and lies down on the couch.

"Your mother got sick with you, and she took afternoon naps."

Gabby needs to change the subject. "I miss you. When are you and Rita coming to visit?"

"Now that you aren't there to help out at the gallery, Rita is swamped with work. We need to wait until things settle down. By the way, Rita sold a few of your paintings." His voice is cheery, and her heart sinks. He continues, "You may want to give her a call. Maybe you could let her know your plans. If you're not coming back to the gallery to work after the baby is born, Rita can hire someone now. It will make work much easier for her."

"I haven't decided yet." She closes her eyes.

"Let us know as soon as possible, kitten."

"I need time to think it all through."

"Gabby, I know that you will make the right decision."

She feels a flutter in her stomach. She has never felt anything like that before. *Is that the baby moving? Is the baby trying to help me make a decision?*

She takes a deep breath and changes the subject again. "How's the campaign going? Is Richard leading in the polls?"

"Yes, he is. Everything is going as planned." King clears his throat. "Have you talked to him yet?"

She wonders how the conversation has come around full circle back to her pregnancy so quickly. "No, Daddy, I haven't talked to him."

"What about Brett? Have you talked to him yet?"

"No, Daddy, I haven't spoken to him either."

"Sorry, kitten. I know it's not easy for you." The softer tone of his voice makes her believe that he understands.

"Daddy, how is Brett?" She closes her eyes and holds her breath as she waits for his response.

"You should be asking him yourself. He's hurting, Gabby. Talk to him."

"It's complicated, Daddy. I do miss him," Her voice quivers.

"I know. He misses you too." There is a long silence. Finally, King says, "Well...Rita and I are driving out to the ranch this weekend. The new furniture is being delivered. Take care, honey."

She hears a click before she has a chance to say good-bye. The conversation has left a gnawing feeling in her stomach. She closes her eyes and remembers her life before coming here. She really misses Brett, and she is starved to hear any news about him. She is reminded of the age-old saying: Absence makes the heart grow fonder. It describes her feelings, but does Brett feel the same? Does he hunger for her as much as she craves him? His previous declarations of love force her to smile for a brief second. If he truly loved her, why hasn't he tried to contact her? She glances down at her phone. The clear screen reminds her that there have been no missed calls. This gives her reason to doubt his love. Maybe he has found someone else. Maybe he is fed up with her foolish behavior.

Yes, her daddy is right. She should have called Brett, and she will. She'll call him after she goes to the adoption agency. Then she'll be able to give him some concrete answers to all the questions he's bound to ask. She'll know more about their chance for a future together after she has made a plan about the baby.

Gabby misses the wide-open spaces in Texas that allow her to see the stars. Here in D.C. there are so many tall buildings and lights that it is nearly impossible for her to get a view of the night sky. She had tried the balcony, but instead of offering her stargazing with a cool breeze, she was hit with a blast of humidity, ambient light, and the noise from the honking of car horns and sirens.

Knowing that the stars are there but invisible to her had given her an idea. She smiles as she remembers how Stan thought her silly as he climbed the stepladder to place the glow-in-the-dark stars on the ceiling of her room. She even made him place them in constellations so she could gaze at the Big Dipper and the North Star. Seeing them comforts her by giving her a feeling of being close to home.

In her bed, stargazing, Gabby rubs her protruding stomach as she feels some movement stirring within. "Hey, little one," she coos. "Do you wish to be a city boy or a country boy?"

Yes, she knows that the baby she is carrying is a boy. Today, at her doctor's appointment, Gabby broke her unwritten rule; she requested the sex of her child. Previously, she had wished to distance herself, thinking that it would make the adoption process easier. However, after reviewing the potential adoption families, many of the applicants requested a specific sex. Gabby shudders, recalling her appointment at the adoption agency earlier this week.

"Hello, Mrs. King. How are you today?" Gabby was greeted by the agent sitting behind the desk at the adoption agency.

The small office was on the fourth floor of a very old building. Her eyes shifted from the floor to the ceiling and then back again. The desk was piled high with manila folders, and wooden shelving along the wall held hundreds more. The files were piled so high that they obscured the view out the window. Some sections of the files were tagged with pink and others were tagged with blue. Some sections had green or white in addition to the pink and blue. Gabby wasn't sure what any of these colored stickers represent.

"We need your medical records to validate the health of your baby," the woman behind the desk said without looking up. Gabby noticed that the off-white folder in front of the woman had no stickers.

"Of course."

"Will you be seeking reimbursement for medical payments?" Gabby knitted her brow and was silent. The agent glanced up from her paperwork. "Some parents will pay all expenses. They want the best for their baby. You can understand that. So, will you be seeking reimbursement for medical costs?"

She shook her head no.

"Are you carrying a boy or a girl?"

She answered with a puzzled look, "I don't know the sex."

"If you've had a sonogram, I can get the sex from your records. Most parents like to know. Some potential candidates request a specific sex. It helps."

She was confused. "How can I decide on parents who request a boy or girl if I don't know the sex?"

The adoption agent answered, "You could pick one set of parents *for a boy and one set for a girl. I'll handle it from there. You won't ever have to know. Do you have any other preferences? Race, religion, that sort of thing?"*

Gabby said, *"I haven't thought about it."*

"Okay, we'll leave that blank for now." The woman looked over the rim of her glasses and continued with the interview. *"The father's first and last name?"* Gabby remained quiet again.

The agent took off her glasses and sat up straight in her chair. *"We really need to have these forms completed before moving forward with the adoption."*

"Okay," Gabby said with a lump in her throat. *"Can I take them home? I didn't know there would be so many things to consider."*

"Bring them back as soon as possible. The sooner you get into the system, the better it is for everyone involved. I'll give you a folder with applicants who are seeking a child. These may help you make some decisions. You can get a feel for what you like." The woman pushed her chair away from the cluttered desk and picked up a folder with a white sticker and handed it to Gabby along with the adoption forms. *"After you narrow it down to two or three candidates, I can make arrangements for you to meet with them. It will help you decide, trust me. I've been doing this for nearly fifteen years. It's not as hard as it seems,"* she said as her hand still held the folder.

"Once you make a decision and see the happiness your baby will bring to a couple who has been waiting, you'll be so relieved. Your baby will be a great blessing. There are so many childless couples." The agent waved her arms to the stack of folders piled behind her. *"There are so many who want a child to love."*

Gabby spoke in a soft whisper, "Even though the baby's not their flesh and blood."

"You'll have nothing to worry about. They'll love your baby. Well, sometimes more than the natural parents." Gabby thought that hard to believe.

She stood. Her knees were weak. She uttered words of thanks to the woman and held the folder to her chest in an effort to hide her rapid heartbeat. Its beating resonated so loudly within her skull that she didn't hear the agent's final words as she made her way out of the office to the elevator.

Gabby did not wish to rule out a proper family for her baby, so for the baby's welfare she had to know the sex. The baby moves again.

"What are you trying to tell me?" she whispers in the dark. She snuggles lower in the down comforter. The stars overhead remind her of the ranch and, right now, she wants the familiarity of her life before coming to D.C.

Now, Gabby continues to stare at her star-lit ceiling. *A boy. A baby boy. My father would be so happy. I could lie and tell Brett that he is the father. Who would know? We could get married and raise the baby on the ranch. We could be a family.* A tear rolls down her cheek. She desperately misses Brett. Trapping him into marriage is wrong. Pretending he is the father is wrong. Gabby hardly recognizes the person she is becoming. The words of the adoption agent play over and over in her mind. If strangers will love her baby, will Brett? She does love her baby. She doesn't know how or when or why, she only knows that she does. If only she could make herself talk to Brett.

Earlier tonight, she and Stan had gone on a double-date with Ella and Will. It was a lovely evening, probably one of the best she'd had since moving here. Dinner was at Les Amies, another French restaurant. It was one that both Stan and Will gave the highest recommendation. Gabby closes her eyes and recalls every detail of the evening.

Stan and Gabby are already seated at the table when Ella approaches them. Gabby gasps. Ella looks grand.

"Ella—hello. Wow, I love your dress!" Gabby stands to hug her best friend. "And I love the way you look in that dress. I should paint a cityscape with you in it looking just the way you do tonight." She leans back to give her friend another look as she holds her at arm's length. Ella's deep pink dress has a high neckline in the front but plunges below her waist in the back. She appears much taller than her short stature with the five-inch silver heels. Her jewelry sparkles but is dim compared to her smile. "But it wouldn't do you justice. You are radiant!"

After Will hugs her, Gabby feels her own expression turning sullen. She glances down at her maternity dress and presses her belly.

"You look just as beautiful, even more so," Stan whispers as he pulls the chair out for her. She feels his breath on her neck. It's as if he can read her thoughts. He places his arm around her waist before brushing his lips on her cheek.

They place their order with the waiter and enjoy their comradery. At first the conversation is light and jovial, but before long, Will asks, "Gabby, are you enjoying the city?"

Gabby lies, "I like it, although it's different from living in Texas."

"I agree with you on that." He lifts his glass as if toasting. "Ella tells me that you had a doctor's appointment today. Is everything moving along as expected?"

Gabby nods. "Yes, it's all good." *Keep your answers short.* She doesn't reveal her news. And for now, the sex of the baby is her secret.

"Have you made a decision…you know, selected parents?" Will shifts his weight in his chair and studies her face. Then she sees that he looks at his brother. She feels the blood drain from her face, and her eyes glance away. She wasn't aware that this topic would be up for conversation. *Take a breath. Relax.*

Stan reaches over and grabs her hand. "Tonight we're here to enjoy and celebrate life. No more questions." He raises his eyebrows at Will. "Let's eat, drink, and be merry."

Stan has saved her from answering, rescuing her once again.

She gives Stan an appreciative smile and squeezes his hand. As the evening continues, she can forget about her pregnancy. Once again their banter is lively. They discuss the news, the latest movies, and some controversial books that have recently made their way to the top of the bestseller list. Stan, in his usual good form, tells jokes and has them all laughing.

The restaurant lives up to its reputation, and after stuffing themselves, they find a downtown club to work off the calories. Gabby watches Ella and Will on the dance floor. Their synchronized movements seem effortless, and she is sure that they aren't aware of anything or anyone other than each other. She sits with her elbows propped on the table, swinging the knot on her necklace back and forth.

"Life isn't over because you're pregnant. You know that," Stan says. "Everything with the pregnancy is normal, right? I thought you were going to faint when Will was firing questions." He pulls her hair back away from her face. This gesture makes her feel exposed and vulnerable. She hasn't shared with Stan her experience at the adoption agency or that she knows the baby is a boy. This small piece of news is her secret and she doesn't wish to share.

He says, "You said your doctor visit was fine. What's going on, Gabby? No bleeding, no cramping, your weight is perfect from what I have been reading."

"Oh, so now you're reading?" Now it was her turn to lift an eyebrow. He has certainly gotten her attention.

"From the literature that I've read," he says with a twinkle in his eye and then pauses to take a sip of wine, "a pregnant woman is able to do everything that she has done previously, in moderation, of course."

With that said, he stands and takes her hand. "Did you dance before you were pregnant?" She's lost in thought as her memories of her first dance with Brett spring forward. It was Valentine's Day and, yes, she danced, her feet were light, and her heart was soaring. Her thoughts are interrupted by the harsh reality that she must have been two weeks into her pregnancy by then.

Stan must have seen her frown and pleads, "It's not a trick question, Gabby. I know you danced."

She looks up at him with wide eyes.

"I saw you dancing at your father's wedding. So, come along." He pulls her up from her chair. "I want to dance, and I know that once I get you swinging to the rhythm, you'll forget about your cares for a while."

She allows him to pull her to her feet, and he leads her to the dance floor close to Ella and Will. Stan winks at them and holds her lightly as he sways to the music. She does enjoy dancing, and she has missed having close intimate contact. Feeling comfortable, she rests her head on his chest and enjoys the sound of the band.

"I'm not making you dizzy, am I?" he asks.

She looks up at him and smiles. "No, it's nice."

"It's nice to see you smile. Your smile lights up the whole room and that makes me happy."

After the music stops, she claps. He pulls her in closer and kisses her on the cheek. Her eyes find the floor. *Is he aware that he's making me uncomfortable?* Without a response, she leads him back to their table where Will and Ella are cuddling. Gabby wonders if they caught sight of Stan's display of affection.

As they approach, Will stands. "It's time to go, big brother. Work will come too soon tomorrow."

Outside the club, the night air is balmy. While Stan waves down a cab, Ella and Will say their goodbyes as they are close enough to walk home. The taxi ride to Stan's condo is smooth because few cars are on the street. Gabby is quiet. He places his arm around her shoulders. "Here, lean against me. You must be tired."

"I am," she says. "But I had a wonderful time. Thank you for a lovely evening." She feels him hold her more tightly.

"It's my pleasure. We'll have many, many more." He rests his chin on the top of her head.

She closes her eyes and enjoys the warmth of his body. *Everything will be all right.*

CHAPTER 12

Back in Texas
King

The main dining room at the country club is packed. It's quite festive with banners hanging from the ceiling, flags jetting from the centerpieces on the tables, and the wait staff dressed in outfits with stars and stripes. The band members wear bright red suit jackets and play uplifting, gay music. It's all very remarkable, King thinks, and it should be since his committee has poured mega-bucks into the Richard Wright for Senate campaign.

King stands with his hands in his pockets, surveying the crowd and taking inventory. He's more interested in who isn't there than who is. He makes a mental note of those missing because he will be calling them for a luncheon date or afternoon drinks in the near future. The admissions are stopped momentarily with a waiting line forming outside the doors as the numbers have reached the fire code limit. All in all, he is pleased with the turnout, and he hopes that the smiling faces mean that the people attending are committed to casting their votes for Richard.

King maneuvers through the crowd and stands next to his candidate.

Richard nods. "Wow, what a great crowd."

"I got them in the door with the free food and drinks; now it's up to you. Woo them and get them into bed. Certainly, you're aware of how critical your presentation is. Do me proud, son."

Richard gives King a thumbs-up and slaps a "Wright is the Right Choice" sticker on his lapel.

The election is still four months away. All of King's oil buddies want Richard to win the Senate seat as much as he does. The current senator is old and has become complacent and hasn't protected their investments as they would have liked, so the oilmen are glad for a new man to take his seat. King has promised them that Richard will be their puppet.

Yes, Richard is his pick for the job. It all started one evening three years ago as King was playing cards. That was the first time he laid eyes on Richard Wright.

"Who's that?" King asked as he shifted his eyes to the well-dressed young man seated at the bar at the country club.

One of the men at the poker table said, "That's the new attorney. He took a job with that big firm downtown, the one on Congress Street. His name is Richard."

"Does he have a last name?" King asked as he shifted the cards in his hand.

"Yeah, Wright, that's it. Imagine, an attorney having the last name

of right." The man chuckled. "What if the judge says he's wrong?" All the men laughed.

"I hear he has a decent golf game. Maybe we should ask him to join us some morning. Get to know him better. It can't hurt to have a lawyer in your pocket."

"A lawyer always finds his way into your pocket. It's getting him out that's the problem." All the men laughed again.

King took a sip of his whiskey. "Our senator is approaching retirement, and we need someone in D.C. It's never too early to start thinking about a replacement." He lifted his glass and from their nods it seemed that the men agreed.

That was the start of their relationship. Within a few weeks, King introduced Gabby to Richard, and it wasn't long before they were living together. Everything was moving along nicely. Well, until Richard did some things, and Gabby didn't turn a blind eye, and they broke up. In hindsight, King thinks it is all for the best that they split. He was tired of seeing Gabby struggle with Richard, so much so that King orchestrated her relationship with Brett.

Suddenly King's ears perk up when he hears Gabby's name mentioned by a group of young women. He moves closer, ever so slightly, to eavesdrop. He recognizes a few of them as being members of Gabby's tennis team.

"Richard is so hot," one of the women says. "And he's single again."

"I thought he and Gabby lived together," a thin, tall brunette says.

"They split, and that's not all. I hear that he calls her a whore. Guess he caught her sleeping around."

"I think he's an arrogant pig. I don't want to deal with that, so he's all yours." A third woman in the group shakes her head back and forth. "Why don't you tell him if he wants your vote, he needs to take you out on a date."

King hears the women laugh. He'll need to have a chat with dear Richard. *How dare he spread rumors about my daughter.*

He surveys the room once again and to his delight Brett is seated the bar. He walks over.

"Hello, Brett."

"Mr. King," Brett raises his glass.

"What brings you here?" King asks.

"After finishing my tennis lessons for the day, I saw all the banners lining the drive to the club, and I was curious to see what was going on. Besides, there's free food and free beer. This is quite a show. My employee badge kept me from waiting in that mob outside the door."

"Are you voting for Richard?"

"Quite the opposite, I don't care for the man. Word has it that you're backing him," Brett says as he points to the sticker on King's lapel.

"I need a man in the Senate to take care of the oilmen in Texas. Richard is the only attorney that I feel I can persuade to vote in our favor." King clears his throat.

"He's such a snake." Brett shakes his head as if in disgust. "I can't figure out why Gabby ever took up with him."

"I've been grooming him for two years. I'm close to having all the pieces in place." He places his hand on Brett's shoulder. "Richard wasn't always this way. He has changed over the years—money and power does that to a person. He thinks he's in control."

Brett takes a swig of his beer.

King takes a seat on the adjacent barstool and explains, "For now, I need Richard to be confident. After he wins in November, he'll find out that he's just a pawn. That's when I'll rein him in and keep him on a shorter leash. Brett, you know Gabby. If Richard had the attitude that he does today, do you really think that Gabby would have been with him? They lived together for almost two years, for Christ's sake."

"You don't need to remind me," Brett says. He taps his fingers on his beer bottle. "These days, I'm beginning to think I don't know your daughter at all."

King starts to speak but before he can get out one word, Brett interrupts, "On second thought, I don't want to know. If she can't tell me herself, then the hell with it all." He stands.

King follows him to the door and says, "Mark my words, everything will turn out. If you love her, be patient."

Brett walks away slowly as if in agony. King shakes his head.

After his conversation with Brett, King studies Richard from across the room. Everything was in place a year ago, nearly perfect until Richard started letting the power go to his head. He became arrogant and foolish and started cheating on Gabby. King had thought if he brought in some competition, Richard would realize the error of his ways and straighten up. That's when King brought Brett into the picture, but instead of giving Richard another chance, Gabby chose Brett and sent Richard walking.

He puts his hands on his hips. He loves his daughter more than anything, but her indecision is driving him crazy. The solution is black-and-white. Why do women tend to complicate and overthink everything? He could have given her advice but knows that it's best for her to figure it out for herself. Can't she see the damage she is causing by hurting Brett and putting their relationship in jeopardy? *Gabby, it's so simple.*

CHAPTER 13

Brett

It's Brett's turn to work the front desk at the tennis club. It's the least favorite part of his job but one he is assigned to several hours each week. The job isn't hard. He answers the phone and books court reservations for members.

Hearing a familiar voice, Brett looks up to confirm what he already knows. Quickly, he turns his attention back to the reservation book. Yes, it is Richard, and he is with Trina, one of the new members. Brett heard that she was recently divorced, and he wonders if Richard is her attorney. She is a beautiful woman, and in the days before Brett started dating Gabby, he would have been sure to spend some time getting to know her.

Taking a deep breath to compose himself, Brett lifts his head and looks Richard in the eye and casually says, "Hello, what can I do for you?"

Brett thinks Richard could have dropped in from London. His white shorts have sharp creases running up the front, and his white polo shirt is neatly tucked in at his waist. It is as if he is dressed to play a match at Wimbledon instead of a social match in the middle of Texas.

"What court are we on, boy?" Richard leans over the desk and gets his face near Brett's. Both of Richard's arms are extended on the wooden surface that separates them.

Brett's fake smile remains painted on his face as he silently counts to ten. *Let it go. Let him be a jerk. Give him the court number, and he'll go away.*

Still looking at the reservation book on the counter, Brett answers, "Court Two."

Richard hasn't moved, and he is still glaring at him. "So, Gabby left you. You weren't right for her. Everyone could see that."

Brett puts his hands on his hips. *You're such a jerk.* "Didn't Gabby leave you first?" The duel is on.

Richard smiles. "I hear she's knocked up. What a whore." He shakes his head from side to side. "Glad I'm through with her."

Brett's eyes widen and his mouth drops open. He has allowed his opponent the first powerful blow. He stands speechless, the color drained from his face and his knees weak.

Richard chuckles. His eyes are bright, dancing in delight.

Richard turns to Trina. "Let's go." He places his arm around her waist, and as they exit the tennis shop, he calls over his shoulder, "Have a nice day, Mr. Tennis Pro."

Brett stares after him. *Gabby's pregnant? Am I going to be a father?* His heart pounds loudly, and he clenches his fists. He should have punched Richard in the face. He has no right to talk about Gabby that way. Perspiration beads on his forehead and his hands are sweaty.

The phone rings unanswered. He sits down, grateful that the shop is empty. What the heck is he going to do?

Brett had dialed Gabby's cell phone several times after he left her sitting in the restaurant, but he never left a message. He was frustrated that she didn't want to live together, and it was his pride that kept him from chasing her. Then, he was furious when she left him the voice message telling him she was leaving.

Now he thumbs through his phone. He hasn't called her in weeks. But in all fairness, she only called twice and left a voice message. They are at a stand-off. He thought they loved each other; he was ready to commit, but Gabby ran. The ball was in her court.

Since then, he has been doing his best to cope. During the day, he pretends that it's business as usual. And after work, he runs and then hits the gym. He's dead tired when he opens the door to his apartment. He eats dinner—usually something out of the freezer or take-out that he picks up on his way home—in front of his television, watching mindless sitcoms.

Once, he tried the bar scene, but he was miserable. Another time, he tried going to a hockey game with some friends, but his thoughts of Gabby prevented him from appreciating the sport. So he gave up, but now, after his confrontation with Richard, things have changed. The game has changed, and he needs a different strategy.

Brett runs his fingers through his hair. *Where is she? Is she pregnant with my child?* This calls for immediate action. He scratches his chin. He might not know where Gabby is, but he knows people who must know. He has played this waiting game long enough. Richard's words keep reverberating in his head, and they spur him to take the matter into his own hands.

He can hardly wait for his shift at the tennis desk to end. He glances at the clock every minute. The hands have barely reached three o'clock, and he is already out of the door, sprinting to his car.

Arriving at Art Smart, Brett storms through the glass doors. On several occasions, he has tried speaking to Rita, and her answer has always been the same. She says, "Gabby loves you. She needs time. Be patient. It will all work out." But this time, he isn't leaving without some answers.

"Rita, Rita," he yells.

She is with a customer.

"I'll be with you in a moment," she says, looking at him. "Brett, honey, help yourself to a sweet tea until I finish with Mrs. Black."

Reluctantly, he walks to the back room of the gallery. He opens the refrigerator and then slams it. He needs answers, not sweet tea. He reopens the door to the fridge and grabs a bottle of his favorite beer and twists off the cap. Gabby kept them for his visits. He tries sitting on the couch, but his legs won't be still, so he's forced to pace back and forth. He chugs the beer, praying to feel the alcohol's numbing effects. Anything would be better than this uneasiness. He doesn't remember the last time he was this angry and felt so betrayed and violated.

Finally, he hears the bells on the gallery door jingle, a signal that the customer is gone. He pinches his lips and overcomes his desire to scream Rita's name once more. He turns around seconds after he hears the click of the door locking, and Rita is facing him with her hands on her hips.

"Where is she?" he yells. He throws his baseball cap down on the couch.

"Lower your voice. There is no need to shout." Rita calmly sits on the couch and motions him to sit next to her.

His nervous rage doesn't allow him to heed her command. He shakes his head and continues pacing. "Where is she?" This time he asks in a more controlled voice, trying his best to keep his temper under wraps.

As he approaches, Rita stands, forcing him to stop pacing. "Give her time. She needs to figure things out."

"She's had plenty of time!" He gives in to his temper again. "I'm not leaving until I know where she is."

"It's not for me to say," Rita explains as she reaches out to rub his arm. "I hate seeing you like this."

He pushes her arm away and continues to pace the length of the room. "Richard came to the club today."

"Oh, was he campaigning?" she asks, lifting her eyebrows.

"Richard says that Gabby is pregnant. Is that true?" The look on Rita's face speaks volumes. "So it really is true. God damn it!" He throws his hands up in the air.

Rita looks out the window. "Like I told you, Brett, it's not for me to say." He hears the uneasiness in her voice. She wrings her hands, then stands and walks in the opposite direction.

"Richard called Gabby a whore. I should have decked him, that son-of-a-bitch." Brett slams his fist into his open hand.

"Oh, my," Rita says. "Brett, you know Gabby. Richard is upset because she picked you instead of him. He's trying to get you riled up, and from what I can see, his plan is working."

121

"God, I despise that man. I'm so mad and so lost." His voice dwindles off and his face drops into his hands.

He hangs his head and lets out a deep breath. "I'm sorry I yelled at you. It's not your fault. I know you are stuck in the middle." He sits on the couch and takes Rita's hands in his own. "Where is she, Rita? I'm so angry and confused. If she loved me, she would be with me, right? If she's pregnant, I have the right to know. Please, tell me where she is. We can work this out."

Rita pats his hand. "She's confused. I can't tell you where she is, but I'll talk to her. I'll let her know that her secret is out. That's the best I can do. I can tell that you want more, and you deserve more." This time, he doesn't push her away and allows her to stroke his arm.

"Maybe the two of you need another one of my lessons on communication. The last one seemed to do the trick." She winks. "I really had hopes that this would have been resolved by now. I wonder what Gabby is thinking?"

"You and me both, Rita. What is going on?"

"Wayne and I are going out to the ranch this weekend. Why don't you spend some time with us? The open space and the fresh air will do you some good." Rita cups her hand on Brett's cheek and says, "We're your family too."

Her reassurance of his place in their family is a welcomed comfort.

He nods his head and looks back up at her. "Thanks, Rita. I would like that. Riding will help. It always has in the past."

Brett loves spending time at the ranch. Even though Rita evaded answering his question, she did invite him to the ranch. Is Rita giving him a clue? Gabby may not be at the ranch, but there is a good chance that someone there may give him some answers. He makes a new plan. He gets in his sports car and puts down the top. First, he'll need to stop briefly at his apartment for a change of clothing, and then he'll be on his way in no time. Besides, the two-hour drive will help him clear the cobwebs from his mind.

He opens the front door to his apartment and packs his clothing in a bag. He's not sure how long his stay will be, but he is prepared for a week. He glances up at the Trinity Knot painting on his mantel. It is Gabby's favorite painting, and he recalls her interpretation. The three loops represent the members of her family, and the circle connecting the loops is the love that unites them. *Where do I fit in all of this?* He shakes his head; then with his duffle bag in hand he locks the door behind him.

The drive to the ranch was indeed the right distraction—the high speeds he drove, though dangerous, were exhilarating. His previous raging fire of anger has turned into smoldering embers that he can manage. After driving through the main gate, he follows the gravel path to the bunkhouse located behind the main house. Rusty is working by the stables, so he cuts the engine and jumps out of the car.

"Hey there, Rusty,"

"Why, Mr. Matthews, what a surprise. King didn't tell me you were coming." Rusty reaches out his hand to shake Brett's. "How are you?"

"Fine, just fine," Brett lies. "Hey, call me Brett, enough of that mister talk."

"What brings you out to the ranch? We're going to be weaning the calves soon. I really could use your help. Let me know your schedule so we can get it on the calendar."

Brett ignores Rusty's question. "Miss Gabby here?"

"No...can't say that she is," Rusty says as he scratches his head and looks puzzled. "Is she back from D.C.?"

Brett smiles and tries to act as normal. But he is so pleased. *Wow, that was easy. So, Gabby's in Washington. Why didn't I think of this before? I could have saved myself weeks of anguish.*

Rusty continues to stare. Unable to look Rusty in the eye, Brett looks down at his feet and kicks the dust back and forth with his boots.

He says, "I've got a request. Well, more of a question. Are you hiring?"

"Depends," Rusty says, shifting his weight from one foot to the other. "Who's asking?" He scratches his chin.

Brett avoids looking at him. "I need a change. The tennis is getting old. I love it here, Rusty. But I need to work."

"You asking me for a job?" Rusty cocks his head to the side.

"Guess I am. I want a job working here." He runs his fingers through his hair and looks out across the horizon. The words were easier said than what he first imagined.

"We'll be weaning the calves in a few weeks. You, son, are the best cattle cutter I've seen in quite a few years." Rusty takes off his hat and wipes his head with the bandana he took from his pocket. "You sure you know what you're doing? It's hard work and long hours, but things do slow down after we get the cattle to market." He replaces his hat back on his head. "Just because you date the boss's daughter doesn't mean I'm going to cut you any slack. Understand?"

Rusty winks at him.

"I wouldn't expect you to."

"Welcome aboard," Rusty says as he shakes his hand. "Wait until Jamie finds out. All she ever talks about is that dimple of yours. Son, don't make me regret hiring you."

"I'll make you proud. Thanks for the job."

"You have perfect timing, kid. Friday evening is always ranch-hand dinner. See you at six p.m. Jamie will be thrilled to see you at the table. Hope you're hungry. She puts on quite a feast."

Rusty starts to walk away but stops and turns. "You can put your things in the bunkhouse. Pick any empty cot. New mattresses are on top." Rusty winks, turns, and continues on his way to the house.

Brett takes his cell phone from his pocket. He dials the tennis club and, surprisingly, at this time of the afternoon the director is still there. "Hello, sir. This is Brett Matthews. I need to take some personal time. I'll work weekends until you can hire my replacement."

Brett listens to the man talking as he watches the sun making its way to the far horizon. Then he says, "Thank you for understanding." He pauses. "Yes, I think Ed will do a great job running my clinics. He's wanted full-time work for a while now." He pauses again. "Thank you, sir. Have a nice weekend." He puts his phone back in his pocket.

Quitting my job was easy. Wow, I just changed my life. It feels good. "Thank you, Richard, you son-of-a-bitch," he mumbles out loud. In just two hours, he has learned that Gabby is in Washington, D.C., and he has landed a new job.

He chuckles and shakes his head. The pieces of the puzzle are finally falling into place. It makes sense because it was Ella who moved to D.C. first. Of course, Gabby went to D.C. She has a problem and then goes to her best friend. That's what women do, right? He will get to the bottom of this. He smiles. *I'm not stupid, Gabby. I know that best friends tell each other everything.* He looks across the horizon once again and whispers, "Gabby, I found you."

Brett turns his thoughts back to the ranch. *I wonder what King will think when he finds out that I'm working on his ranch.* He grabs his gear from the passenger seat, throws it over his shoulder and whistles as he walks to the bunkhouse. The heavy cloud that surrounded him for the past few weeks is finally lifting.

After picking out a bunk and stowing his gear, Brett meanders to the main house for dinner. He hears the laughter and talking long before he opens the door to see the ranch hands all gathered around the large table. Jamie is carrying out platters of meats and bowls of vegetables and setting them on the table.

Upon seeing him, Jamie squeals, and then she runs over to him and gives him a big hug.

"Mr. Matthews, Mr. Matthews, I can't believe it's you." She pinches his cheek. "Rusty says you're going to be working here. My, my, wait til' Miss Gabby..." Her voice trails off. "Please forgive me. I shouldn't have." She covers her mouth with her hand.

Brett takes her by the arm. "Jamie, I know that she's in D.C."

"I'm sorry. I shouldn't have said anything." She reaches up and touches his face. "You're a good boy. I pray every night that it will all work out." She turns away. *What does Jamie mean by that?*

After the meal, some of the cowboys sit around the table drinking coffee while others head home to their families for the weekend. As Jamie retreats to the kitchen carrying a tray of dirty dishes, Brett pushes back his chair. When he's sure no one is watching, he makes his way up the curved staircase. The door to Gabby's room is open. He hesitates before entering and takes a deep breath. Ever so slowly, he enters, and then he closes his eyes. The room smells as if she were right there. *Gabby, why did you leave? Talk to me. We can get through this. I love you, you silly girl.*

He walks over to the vanity and picks up the crown Gabby had won at the rodeo when she was fourteen. He recalls the selfie they took on the day of Rita and King's wedding. On that day, he placed this crown on her head. *God, she was beautiful. That day we were so happy. What happened? Why didn't she tell me that she was pregnant? Sure, we aren't ready to be parents but we could discuss it. Does she think I wouldn't be a good father?*

Looking around the rest of the room for more clues as to Gabby's mysterious behavior, Brett pulls his finger through the dust on the dresser. No one has been in this room in weeks. Next, he opens the closet filled with her shirts and jeans. There hangs her favorite blue dress. He pulls the soft fabric to his nose and breathes deeply, inhaling her lingering scent. The garment smells of her favorite Chanel perfume—a scent he has grown to love. Her cowboy boots are on the floor. *I guess she doesn't need these in the city.*

He searches the room again in hopes of finding more clues that could shed some light on the reason Gabby left town. He reaches for her crocheted blanket since it is one of her favorite things and clutches it to his chest. While bending to look out the window, he sees the evening star and makes a wish. *Is she wishing on that same star?*

A voice speaks, startling him. He turns to find Jamie smiling at him. "I'm glad you're here. I know you love her." He looks down at the blanket and places it back on the bed. "I think of you as a part of this family. We all do, Brett."

"I was just..." he says, trying to explain. He rubs his forehead.

"I know. It's okay." He can hear the sympathy in her voice and see it in her kind gestures. "You could write her a letter. Tell her you miss her. Tell her you love her. She can read it over and over. Trust me. Women of all ages like love notes. I'll make sure she gets it." She turns and is gone.

He is alone with his thoughts. *Nobody writes letters anymore. But I'm desperate.* He needs the help and support of others. He is thankful that Jamie has offered to help and seems to be on his side. Sitting at the small desk, he opens the top drawer where there is a tablet. He rips out a sheet of paper and finds a pen. What more does he need to say than I love you?

CHAPTER 14

Gabby

Gabby is only a few blocks from the Metro station in downtown Arlington, a Virginia suburb across the Potomac River from Washington. She fumbles with the map, turning it upside-down. Where did she make a wrong turn? She squints at the name on the street sign. The heat from the bright sun radiates off the sidewalk. She frowns as she realizes that she took the north exit out of the subway instead of the south exit, making her journey twice as long. She was never good with maps. She wipes her brow. *Darn this humidity. My hair will frizz, and my puffy feet are already screaming in these heels. I should have worn my flats.*

She wished to look her best for the interview at the Crystal Art Gallery. Stan had arranged the interview through one of his friends. It will be good for her to work and to have a goal other than watching the calendar, counting the days until her due date, which is circled in bright red. Turning around, she walks the few blocks back to the Metro station, and she starts on her journey again.

The Crystal Art Gallery is one of the shops located in a row of brick buildings on the historic town's main street. Looking into her reflection in the gallery front window, she adjusts her dress and smoothes her hair. She studies the compositions and color schemes of the landscape paintings displayed in the window, thinking them decent. She checks her cell phone for the time and quickly throws the phone in her purse. *Put on your happy face,* she tells herself. *You need to appear confident and competent.*

Upon opening the door, she is greeted with the familiar jingle of bells. Glancing up in the direction of the sound, she finds two small silver bells tied with blue string attached to the door. The bells remind her of Art Smart Gallery in Texas. Is this an omen?

"Hello," a female voice calls from a chair in the far corner. The woman closes the book she is reading. "Can I help you?" She stands and walks toward Gabby.

Gabby clears her throat, "I'm looking for Janet Crystal."

"You must be Miss King. Right on time," She looks at the clock on the wall. "I like punctuality."

Gabby guesses Ms. Crystal's age to be about sixty. She has a kind, round face that fits with her plump figure.

"Please, call me Gabby." She shakes the woman's hand.

"I will, but only if you call me Janet." Laughing, she motions to the chairs. "Please have a seat."

Gabby sits down and sighs. Her dress clings to her wet body.

"My dear, you looked flushed. The weatherman predicted higher than average temperatures. For once, his prediction is correct. Let me get you some cold water." Janet returns with the glass.

"Thank you. I like the warm weather, but I'm not used to this humidity." Gabby holds the cold glass against her arm.

"I understand that you are from Texas," Janet says. "What brings you to Washington?"

Gabby pauses. *How much do I need to say?* "I needed a change," she stammers, wringing her hands. "I'm staying in town for a few months."

Janet cocks her head to the side. "Yes, my son mentioned that you were staying with Stan. He's such a nice boy."

Gabby nods her head in agreement, then takes another sip of water.

Janet motions toward the portfolio Gabby has in her lap. "Show me what you have there. I went to your website, but artwork shows much better in person."

Gabby feels her body relax as she begins to describe her abstract impressionism. She talks about each painting as she retrieves it from her folder.

Janet leans forward and asks questions. She seems genuinely interested in hearing about her inspirations and motivations.

"Oh, my, where has the time gone?" Janet says. "We've chatted the afternoon away. I really like your work. It's different from the other abstract work that I have exhibited here before; however, times are changing." She crosses her arms. "My artist for next month canceled two days ago. Can you be ready to exhibit that soon? It only gives you three weeks to prepare. I got the call just this morning, and with your appointment scheduled for this afternoon, I was keeping my fingers crossed that we could help each other."

Gabby's eyes widen. "Really?" she stammers. "I mean, yes, of course. Thank you."

"Contemporary art is the hottest art selling. All the interior designers are staging houses with it, and corporations are purchasing more modern pieces for their lobbies. The current movement is away from the vibrant dark abstracts to those that are softer, creating a warmer atmosphere. If it's good by you, I will email a few photos of your work to our mailing list." Janet stands and reaches for the calendar on her desk.

"That would be great."

"The sneak preview may prompt buyers to attend your reception, so…let's pick some dates?"

Gabby is speechless. This interview has gone more smoothly than she could have imagined. It was different from her past experiences with galleries in the East.

"Why do you seem so surprised? My dear, you're in a city that takes pride in being up to date in the latest trends. You aren't in Texas anymore."

Gabby completes the required paperwork. Then she thanks Janet one more time before she opens the gallery door to leave. The two silver bells clang, and she thinks their sound is a happy one. She walks toward the Metro with a spring in her step. Shaking her head, she mumbles, "You're right, Janet. I'm not in Texas anymore. And I'm not in New York City, either."

Gabby clearly remembers her difficulty marketing her abstract artwork in New York's SoHo district a few years ago. The words of rejection still burn. *"I'm sorry, Ms. King. We're looking for a fresh, new style, something edgy." One gallery door after another closed, and Gabby, frustrated and lonely, returned to Texas.*

However, today she smiles. In a few short weeks living here in

Washington, she is having an exhibition. All the work she has done since arriving here will be gracing the walls of the Crystal Art Gallery.

The three-week deadline will be pressing, and there is so much to do. But first, Gabby places a call to Rita; after no answer she leaves a voice message. However, she is able to get through to Ella.

"Hey, Gabby, how are you? Will and I enjoyed having dinner with you and Stan."

"We enjoyed it too. I'm so happy for you, Ella. I know how long you've waited for a man to sweep you off your feet. It seems that you and Will are the perfect couple."

"Hey, you and Stan make such a cute couple. You know, I think Brett is all that hot and sexy, but really, Gab, when it comes down to a stable guy that you can count on, Stan gets my vote. The way he looks at you and protects you, it's really sweet. He doesn't have Brett's looks, but his personality is great. He would be loyal so you wouldn't ever have to worry about him playing around. Just a little food for thought. I know that your life is on hold until the baby is born."

"Thanks for the advice," Gabby says with distance in her voice as she thinks about Brett. She misses him. Why hasn't he tried to find her? Ella's right. Stan has been supportive but, given the chance, could Brett act in a similar manner? *God, why can't I make a decision and go on with life?*

Ella continues, "Gabby, I know it's a struggle for you. And I also know that you will make a good decision. Okay? But Brett is Brett. He won't sit and mope around forever. Since he hasn't tried to contact you, maybe he has moved on already."

If she allows herself to go down that line of thinking, she could really get depressed. Brett's past history as the club's playboy bothers her. If he chose to stay with her, would he be faithful? She steers away from the painful subject of talking about Brett.

"The reason I called is to tell you some fabulous news." Gabby's voice perks up. "I got a show. The gallery in Arlington liked my work, and I show next month."

"Wow, that's fantastic. Congratulations. Are you having your work shipped here from Texas?"

"No, I'm going to exhibit all of the new stuff I've painted since coming to D.C., my modern pastel abstracts, and my Zeppelin Bend series. It's exciting."

"That's great news. Text me the dates so I can get it on my calendar. Work has been super busy, so I need to run, but let's have lunch soon. Bye."

The loud click confirms that Ella is gone. It lightens her spirit to talk about her art. She would rather share news of the upcoming exhibit, instead of talking about her pregnancy or relationships, especially those that concern either Stan or Brett. This is what she needs, and she's thankful for Stan's connections, which started the wheel turning to get this gig. But Ella made a good point that is hard for Gabby to ignore. Brett isn't the kind of guy to hang around. Since she hasn't heard from him, did he move on?

Gabby hears Stan's key turn in the lock, and she greets him at the door to the condo. She takes his helmet and gloves and then waits with her hand reached out to accept his leather jacket. He smells of oil, and his fingers have grease under the nails. He removes his leather riding boots, then she hands him a beer. Stan grins.

She speaks first. "How was work?"

"Good, it's really hot out there for this early in the summer." He takes a large swig of beer. "This is good, thank you. Wow, something smells awesome. What's for dinner?"

"Something special," she answers as she twirls around in front of him. She proudly beams. "I hope you like it."

"If you made it, I love it, even if I don't," he teases, a twinkle in his eye.

He cocks his head to one side. "What's up? I see a smile on your face. Something is going on."

"We're celebrating."

He turns toward the living room but is stopped by the numerous canvases laid out on the floor. "Whoa, what's all this?"

"It's the reason we are celebrating."

"That's right, I forgot, you had your interview today at the Crystal Gallery. How did it go?"

She claps her hands together and jumps up and down. "My exhibit goes up in three weeks."

"That's exciting. I'm happy for you, Gabby. This is great news."

Her mood becomes more serious. "I need to rush the framing. Janet, the owner of the gallery, is so nice. I really like her. She thinks that my modern abstracts should sell well here."

He takes another swig of his beer. "That's fantastic. See, moving here has its advantages."

"Thank you for making this happen. I am ever so grateful."

"I had a small part." He lifts his bottle up in the air. "It was your art that closed the deal."

Gabby bites her upper lip. "I know I haven't been easy to live with. I'm moody and distant and..." Her hands automatically go to her stomach.

"Hey, stop putting yourself down. You've been great. I love having you here."

"I want you to know, I'm grateful. I can't thank you enough." She feels tears welling up in her eyes, and she cannot bear to look at him. She turns so he cannot see her wipe her eyes. Part of her wants to run into his arms. She has fantasized about how his kiss would feel. He is kind and generous and thoughtful. Maybe Ella is right. Maybe Stan is more stable than Brett.

Yes, she is grateful for everything that Stan has done, but she doesn't love him. *With time, could I learn to love him?* Without thinking, her hand grasps her trinity knot necklace. *Brett, where are you? Why haven't you tried to contact me? Are we over?*

Gabby watches as Stan gingerly steps over a few canvases to get to the couch. He sways a little. She yells, "Be careful!"

"Why do you have all of these canvases all over the floor?"

"I'm getting ready for the show, silly. And I need your help."

He raises his eyebrows as he sits on the couch. "You need my help. How can I possibly help?"

"I'm glad you asked. Each painting needs a title. We're not eating until each one is given a name." She points to the three-by-five cards on the coffee table. "Grab a pen. Start anywhere you want and write a name on the card and then place it on the canvas."

Biting the end of her pen, Gabby thinks, *I'd rather be writing boys' names down on these cards.* There was a time not too long ago when she considered her paintings her babies. She sighs at first but then smiles. *But now I have a real baby to think about. What if I gave these paintings names of boys? That would be silly and totally crazy.*

Gabby crawls on her knees and holds up one canvas after another, turning them as she tries to determine if the composition is more appealing as a vertical or a horizontal. With abstract art, it is subjective. After she gives names to three of the canvases, "Break of Day," "Serenity," and "Wishing," she notices that Stan's card is blank, and a frown has replaced the smile he wore earlier.

Noticing her stare, he says, "I can't do this, so I guess I'll just starve. It smells so good, and I'm so hungry."

"You poor baby," she says, thinking he looks and sounds so sorrowful. "Okay, okay, just one title now, and then after we eat, we can name the rest before having dessert. How does that sound?" He looks at her in disbelief.

"You're such a softie. Do you always give in so easily?" He chuckles and winks at her. "All right, just one." He peers at the canvases on the floor. "I pick this one." He points to a canvas that has dominant yellow hues and a band of muted tones of blue that fades into green. Flecks of gold leaf give the painting a sense of richness. After placing his beer on the coffee table, he writes on the card. Then, he hands the card to Gabby. "Here you go, my one title."

"See, I knew you could help me."

Gabby reads his writing out loud, "'Light of My Life.' Stan, tell me what you see in this painting to support this title."

"You," he quips. "I can see my life with you in it, bright and happy."

What am I to say? Speechless, she lowers her eyes.

Breaking the silence, he says, "You're not taking this one to the gallery."

"And why not?" She makes her voice sound light, forcing herself to look at him.

"Because it's already sold." He proudly retrieves the canvas and heads down the hallway toward his bedroom.

"Where are you going with that?" she yells.

"I'm going to put this in a safe place," he calls back over his shoulder.

"Don't be long. You earned your dinner." *He is so kind. Any girl would be lucky to have him by her side.*

After dinner, Stan and Gabby return to the living room to continue naming the canvases.

Stan holds up a canvas. "You like it better this way or this way?" he asks as he turns the canvas one-hundred-eighty degrees.

"I don't know. What do you think?" She places her hand on her chin in deep thought.

"This one reminds me of a bird." He holds it vertically. "A crippled bird."

"Oh, really? How is that?" She wrinkles her nose and searches the canvas in an attempt to visualize the bird.

"See this?" He points to the canvas. "Here is the body, and here is one wing, but where is the other? Hence, a crippled bird." He laughs and laughs.

His laugh is contagious, and she starts laughing with him.

"Can you please be serious?" she says, smiling through tears of joy.

He plops down next to her on the couch. "I am being serious. It's a crippled bird."

They both laugh again.

"Dinner was great, and chocolate-chip cookies and milk, ahhh, heaven," he says as he takes another bite of his cookie. He leans back into the couch with both hands across his lap.

Gabby reaches down to rub her swollen feet. "I'm glad we got the canvases named. For a while there I thought the project was doomed. Thank you for helping—you made it fun."

"Thank you for dinner. We make a great team. Here, allow me." He lifts her feet up on his lap. "Remember, the doctor said that you are to elevate your feet twice a day. Have you done that today?"

"No, I haven't. It's been a busy day."

"Somebody needs to look after you. That's my job." He winks.

"Oh, oh—" she moans and sits up straight.

"Am I hurting you?"

His concerned look makes him look younger. "No, it's not you. That feels great. It's the baby. He's moving."

He asks, "Can I feel? I've never had the chance."

She smiles as she takes his hand and places it on her belly. "Just wait. He'll do it again."

"You said him. It's a boy? You know?" He raises his eyebrows.

She nods her head. She has accidentally shared her secret. She delights in the way Stan's eyes light up as he feels the baby kick. "Wow, that's a first for me. It must be amazing having the opportunity to grow a new life inside of you."

Then he says, "If you want to have natural childbirth, I can take Lamaze classes with you."

Her mouth drops open. "Did I hear you right? You just offered to take Lamaze classes with me?" She sits up with both hands on her hips.

Stan looks sheepish. "Yes, I've been reading and you need a coach. I can do that. But only if you want to."

"It's a little early; we have a few months. I'll consider it," she says and winks at him. "That's very kind of you. Thank you."

She leans back and notices how she fits snugly into Stan, and he gives her shoulders a squeeze. His warmth feels nice, and this closeness makes her realize that she misses having intimacy in her life. She has missed Brett's kisses and his embrace. As if reading her mind, Stan softly strokes her arm and gives a little hum. Should she give up on Brett? A tear escapes and runs down her cheek. She brushes it away quickly.

Later that night, lying in her bed, Gabby looks at the constellations on the ceiling and thinks about making a wish. Earlier this evening with Stan, she allowed her mind to think about love. She has avoided thinking about love, since it opens a dark place and makes her sad. Her heart beats in her ears, and her head drops. Has she been unfair to Brett? Would Brett have been there for her and the baby? She hasn't given him a chance. She was a coward and ran. She loves Brett so much that she didn't want him to disappoint her. She loves him so much that she couldn't face that he might leave her.

On the other hand, now that her relationship with Stan is developing, is she being unfair to Stan? Is she leading him on? There she was tonight snuggled up against him, allowing him to feel the baby kick. By moving here, she has traded one set of problems for another. God, she is pathetic!

CHAPTER 15

Gabby

"Gabby, it's Rita, pick up. It's important," Rita leaves a message as her call goes to voice mail.

Gabby was going to let the phone ring since she is painting. She has paint all over her hands; however, after she hears Rita's desperate plea, she grabs a towel, starts wiping her hands, and scrambles to reach her phone.

"Hi, Rita, sorry, I couldn't get to the phone sooner. I'm painting."

"Can you talk?" There is urgency in her voice.

"Sure, what's wrong?" Gabby continues to wipe the paint off her fingers.

"There's something you need to know."

"Is everything all right with Daddy?" Her body stiffens and her voice is shaking with fear.

"No, no, sweetie—I mean, yes, your daddy is just fine. It has to do with you."

"Me?" Gabby exhales and switches the phone to her other ear and chuckles. "I'm doing fine. The baby's fine." She begins to relax.

Rita says, "I really don't know where to begin."

Gabby's attempts to relax were premature, and she tenses her shoulders again.

"You're getting me concerned. What's going on?"

"Are you sitting down?"

"No, should I be?"

"It might make it easier."

"Spill it, Rita. What's up?" Gabby puts her hands on her hips. She hears Rita take a deep breath.

"Brett quit his job at the country club."

"Why would he do that?" Gabby bites her upper lip. "I thought he loved working there."

"I don't know exactly, but what I do know is that Richard had a hand in it."

"Richard—oh, no! Did Richard get Brett fired?"

"No, but they had some kind of confrontation at the tennis club."

"About what? Me?"

"I don't know, but there's more."

"I'm listening." Her voice is quiet. She pulls up a chair as her legs are weak.

Rita says, "Later that same day, Brett drove to the ranch and asked Rusty for a job."

"Brett's working for Daddy? None of this makes sense. Why would he give up his job teaching tennis?" Growing more confused, Gabby shakes her head. "Rita, are you sure? I can't imagine Brett quitting his job. There must be a mistake. Did he get fired?"

"I can't answer that but there's more. While at the club, Richard told Brett that you're pregnant."

"Richard knows? How did he find out?" Gabby feels light-headed and the hand holding the phone starts to shake.

"I don't have a clue."

"So you're telling me Brett knows that I'm pregnant?"

"I'm really sorry. I know that you were trying to avoid all of this."

"When did all this happen?"

"This weekend. After Richard had spoken to Brett, Brett came to the gallery demanding that I tell him where you were. Of course, I didn't, but it seems someone did." Rita pauses and takes another breath. "Brett knows that you're in Washington. He told me, so I know that it isn't hearsay."

Gabby's head is spinning. She's trying to digest all this new information.

"Jamie mailed Brett's letter the next day," Rita says. "What did you tell him?"

"What letter?" She scratches her head. "Rita, I don't know anything about a letter."

"The letter that Brett wrote," Rita says. "Gabby, this whole situation is getting messy. Time is running out. The only good thing about all of this—"

"Good thing? How can there be a good thing? This conversation has been one problem after another."

"Richard doesn't know that he is the father."

She sighs in relief. *Okay, that is a good thing.* But her thought is interrupted.

"Brett believes he's the father. You can't let him go on thinking that. You need to talk to him. I understand that you need time, but everything is unraveling." Rita pauses and takes a deep breath. "Your father helps Richard with the campaign, and he is doing his best to keep the news of you and the baby out of the press. Bad gossip will hurt Richard's campaign. Now, there's the problem with Brett. I don't know how much longer we can keep a lid on this."

"Oh, my, I had no idea." Gabby holds her head in her hands and bends over, pierced by the emotional pain. Her heart skips a beat. Her stomach hardens. *What am I to do?*

Rita asks, "Have you made a decision about the baby?"

"Oh, Rita, it's a boy. I'm going to have a boy. Daddy will be overjoyed. He never got the son he wanted, but I can give him a grandson."

"Wait, I thought you weren't going to find out the sex. What has changed?"

"The adoption agency needs to know the sex of the child for placement. I felt like I was limiting my choice of parents by not knowing the sex, and then when I found out—"

Rita interrupts, "It was too late."

"It's a boy—a boy to carry on the King name. Daddy can teach him how to ride and rope. It could be a beautiful thing. I know that it isn't perfect since Richard is the father, but I can't give my baby up for adoption. I thought that I could. I tried talking myself into it, but I can't and I won't."

"Well, then you have made at least one decision," Rita pipes. "When are you telling Brett? The sooner the better."

Gabby sits in silence, swinging her trinity knot on its chain.

"Gabby, when are you telling Brett that he's not the father?"

"Honestly, I really don't know, Rita," Gabby says. "But soon, I promise."

"Everything is unraveling. I won't lie to him. That boy is like a son to me."

"I'm so sorry. I never meant for any of this to happen. I don't expect you to lie."

"Tell him, sweetie. Just tell him. You'll feel so much better. Trust me on this."

CHAPTER 16

King

Well, well, you know what time it is?" King asks.

Richard shakes his head and starts to open his mouth.

"It's a rhetorical question. Don't say a word. I ask myself, why is my phone ringing? I have to haul my ass out of bed during my beauty rest. Then, I hear your name…my political candidate." King raises his voice another decibel. "My candidate is in jail. Four months before the election, and you get your ass thrown in jail."

He takes his Stetson off his head and paces back and forth in the small cell. Then he continues his soliloquy. "This is the big time for you. I hand you the election on a silver platter. It's yours for the taking, and then you do something stupid." He scratches his head.

Richard is sitting on the small metal bench in the jail cell. His eyes are red and glassy. "I didn't mean to—"

"Shut up, I'm not finished." King paces back and forth. "Now it's up to me to fix it. I should let you rot in here. If it were just my ass on the line, I would. Your career would be over. But all of us oilmen need a voice in the Capitol. We thought you were our man, smart and polished. What's happened to you?"

Richard stands. "It was a—"

King pushes hard on Richard's shoulder, forcing him back down on the bench. "Sit down. Did I ask you to speak? You need to pull yourself together and fast."

Richard hangs his head.

"Times like this make me realize that my daughter was wise to tell you to hit the road. When are you going to control your temper and learn to shut that trap of yours? I'm getting tired of your name coming up in a derogatory fashion." He stares at Richard, pointing his finger. "You speak badly of my daughter."

"Did poor Brett run to you? What a loser." Richard's voice is stronger.

"Poor Brett hasn't said a word to me. He does his job and keeps to himself. If you and he were in the same ring, I'd bet all of my money on him. That's why it's killing me to throw my money away to get you out of this little jam you managed to get yourself into."

King looks at his watch and shakes his head. "So let's get down to business. No charges have been filed, yet. You want my help or not? It comes with a price."

"As all things do." Richard bites down hard on his lip without looking up at King.

"I can make this go away, and you can go on with your campaign as if nothing ever happened. You like that?"

Richard nods his head.

"Here's what it takes," King demands. "You're never to come near my daughter or her baby again. Easy, right?"

King glares at Richard and points his forefinger. "You give me your word. I'll kill you myself if you ever do. Understand?"

Richard's face is puzzled. "That's it, stay away from Gabby?" He looks down. "Hell, I moved on months ago."

King adds, "And her baby?" He wishes he could read Richard's face to put validation to his answers, but Richard continues to avoid his stare.

Richard asks, "And her baby?" He doesn't understand King's demands. "You want to add Brett to that list?"

"Don't get smart with me," King says. "Brett can take care of himself. He could beat the crap out of you." He turns to leave. "I'm gonna go and get a bundle of cash out of my account and give it to some lowlife to heal his bruises. Learn to keep your trap shut and stop drinking. Christ, act like a politician." King is still mumbling as he exits.

Richard watches him amble around the corner out of sight.

Richard

Richard wonders what is really going on. The demands King made seem odd. *Does King know I lied? How can I possibly stay away from the woman I love?* Richard clenches his jaw and shakes his head. These past few months without Gabby have been tough. He knows the root of his anger that leads him down this path of destructive behavior. Gabby's pregnancy was a shock. He hates Brett.

An hour later, the door to the jail is opened by the guard, and

Richard sees his nod. The guard speaks. "Mr. Wright, you're free to go. There's a cab waiting out back. No charges were filed." The officer hands him his wallet and watch.

As he climbs into the back seat of the cab, he can't believe that his troubles have disappeared. He wishes his inner turmoil was as easy to fix.

CHAPTER 17

Gabby

H ello, Daddy!" Gabby reaches out to give him a hug. "This is the best surprise ever. I didn't expect you until my reception. I've missed you so much."

"Kitten, not nearly as much as I've missed you." He holds her back at arm's length. "Look at you, a vision of loveliness."

Conscious of her belly, Gabby places her hands on either side. "There's no hiding it," she says.

"You shouldn't have to. You're glowing. How do you feel?"

"I'm feeling great. After I had dealt with the shock and the initial morning sickness, I was surprised to find that I like being pregnant. It's fun to feel the baby moving and kicking."

"Wonderful, wonderful. Where's Stan? I thought he would be here."

"I thought so too, but then he sent me a text and said that he couldn't get the time off work. You'll get to see him tomorrow." She reaches around his waist again. "I get you all to myself!" They walk arm in arm.

Gabby and her father ride the Metro to the main street in Arlington. She wants to show him the art gallery and introduce him to Janet. Afterward, they eat at a quaint Italian restaurant across the street. It is a humid summer evening, one that is typical for this time of the year.

"It was great to meet Janet. She seems nice," King says. "I also like the location of the gallery. It's right in the middle of a commercial area, near the Metro and City Hall. There should be lots of pedestrian traffic; it's a great location, near the big city but with a small-town feel."

After the waiter takes their orders, King takes off his reading glasses and leans forward. "Gabby, there is something we need to discuss."

"Oh, this sounds serious." She takes a sip of water.

"Fill me in on what you've decided. Then I'll tell you my news. Sound like a good trade?"

"Okay." She leans back in her chair. "I decided to keep the baby. I went to the adoption agency, and it seemed all so...so casual. I tried looking at the parent folders, but picking the perfect couple wasn't happening. I felt that nobody could take care of my baby as well as I could. I want the best for him."

King's ears seem to perk up. "Rita told me as much. You said *him*, I heard you." He gives her a wink.

"It's a boy, Daddy. We'll have a wonderful time raising him on the ranch. It makes me giddy just thinking about all of his firsts: his first time to ride a horse, his first time to raise a calf, his first time to swim and to fish, and...it will be so much fun." She pauses and looks deep into his eyes. "You know, if it were a girl, I would have named her Anna, for sure." She looks up at King, searching his face for approval.

"My dear, sweet Anna, she would have been so happy to learn of this news. I miss her, and I know that you do too."

His answer pleases her. She has feared that since he married Rita his memory of her mother would be lost. Just the mere mention of Anna's name triggers her to touch her necklace and swing the knot on its chain.

"Good, I knew you would make the right decision. I'm proud of you, kitten." He reaches across the table and squeezes her hand. "Now, there's the issue of Richard."

Gabby's mouth turns down.

"I think you'll be pleased with what I have to tell you. You came here so that Richard wouldn't get wind of your pregnancy. However, cat's out of the bag on that one. In the meantime, Richard got himself into a heap of trouble."

She gasps. "What kind?"

"It's not important what he did, but what is necessary for you to know is that in exchange for making his little infraction go away, he promised to leave you and the baby alone."

"Does he suspect that he is the father?"

"Not from what I can tell. That brings up another issue. You haven't asked me how Brett is doing." She sees empathy for Brett in her daddy's eyes.

She's relieved that the waiter has come with their dinners. It gives her time to think about her answer. *Daddy's right. I should have asked.* "How is Brett?"

"He's hurting, Gabby. He has been patient and understanding. More understanding than I would ever be if I were in his shoes. You should have answered his letters." He forks food into his mouth.

"Rita said the same thing." She looks up. "I never got a letter."

"Is it possible that Stan intercepted them? Rita tells me he has feelings for you. It would be to his advantage to have Brett out of your life."

"Stan would never do such a thing."

"Are you sure?" King asks, raising his eyebrows. "I had the letter tracked, and it was delivered."

"Interesting," she says thoughtfully, avoiding looking at him.

"Brett's a hard worker. He keeps his nose down, does his work well. He started training for the local rodeo. You should see him ride."

Gabby senses the pride in her daddy's voice, and he is looking at her as if he is waiting for a reply, but she remains silent.

"Kitten, he asks about you every day. Jamie, Rusty, Rita, and I are doing our best to keep him under control but you, dear, are pushing it. This is where I get to give some fatherly advice." He puts his fork down on his plate, and she knows that she is going to be given a lecture.

"Now that I took care of Richard, he won't be bothering you or asking any questions. It is safe for you to come home and tell Brett about the baby. He's level-headed, and he loves you. I know you love him. I see it when you are together. Everybody can see it."

Between bites of his dinner, he continues, "That brings up another discussion. The ranch is the perfect place to raise the baby. You just said it yourself. You know that spot over by the lake where you always have picnics?" He has a gleam in his eye. "I'll build you a house. I know a great architect. You meet with him, tell him what you want, and the house could be finished before the end of the year."

Her eyes are wide, and she has difficulty swallowing. "Sounds as though you have this all figured out."

154

"I want the best for you and my grandson. Besides, that boy needs to be born in Texas. He will be a fifth-generation Texan. Certainly, you weren't thinking of having the baby here?" He looks up at her as he flails his arm in the air. "No way. My grandson will be a Texan. This is not up for debate, my dear."

In her struggle to decide the fate of her little one, Gabby hasn't thought that far into the future. She recalls stories of many women who had left the state of Texas and then returned home just to deliver so that the generation line wasn't broken. Time is moving along quickly. Yes, it will please her daddy for the baby to be a Texan.

She cocks her head to the side and smiles. She really loves this man. He has a spirit and a loyalty that are hard to find among the younger generation. She knows that he only wants the best for her and, now, her baby.

King continues to plead his case. "Texas has been good to our family. It's a good life. I look around here with all of the concrete and the glass. This is no place to raise a child."

"Your point is well taken. I think about my own childhood. It was perfect; I played from the time the sun came up until it set in the evening. I loved the horses and cattle. I loved the open fields, and the flowers in the springtime were the best. I still love everything about Texas." She reaches across the table to clasp his hand. "You may be right about building a house. Let me think about it. Okay?"

He squeezes her hand. "Of course I'm right." He winks. "I'll have the architect send over a few plans. You can get a feel for a few designs. There's lots of land, so if you decide to have a dozen kids, we can always expand." He chuckles.

"First, I need to get this one out before thinking about having more. Besides, I think I would need a husband for that kind of expansion."

"Ah, Gabby, yes, a husband...do you want me to take care of that too?" He looks across the table and winks. "That will be an easy task. I know just the guy."

"No, Daddy, I am perfectly capable. Your help is not needed. Don't you go around meddling." She waves her finger at him.

"Just kidding. I have my own meddling to do and that starts with the lobbyist tomorrow. It seems he needs a little persuasion. I got wind that he hasn't secured enough votes in the committee for Congress to vote in our favor." King leans back in his chair. "Once I get Richard into office, he can look out for the oilmen, and it will save me from taking care of business such as this. Lord knows, we've invested enough in Richard. He'd better come through."

Hearing Richard's name wipes her smile away. Is it possible that he will leave her and the baby alone? Her dad seems hopeful that Brett will accept her baby, which leads her to believe that she and Brett can have a life together. Isn't that her dream? Her daddy is so confident that they have a future together. Have they spoken?

CHAPTER 18

Brett

The time has come for weaning the calves from their mothers. This requires a cowboy who is skilled in cutting. When Brett was a young teen, he was one of the best. Now that he has been practicing for the local rodeo, he knows he hasn't lost his touch. He was a little rusty at first, but he is glad that the old Brett, the one who won the trophies seventeen years ago, is back.

He smiles as he recalls his first two trips to the ranch. King invited him to the barbecue. It was that weekend that Brett and Gabby made their first serious connection. Then, he was able to make a real impression with King when he was here for the branding of the calves. He has great respect for King. *He reminds me of my dad,* Brett thinks.

He stands with one foot propped on the corral's fence rail. Earlier the sun had been hot. And even though the dust is flying, it hasn't gone anywhere and seems to be stuck in the tiny holes of the fabric of his shirt and jeans. He is dirty and smells of old sweat. It only took twelve hours to get all of the calves separated from their mothers.

He is tired, but it is a good feeling. It is altogether different from the tiredness he felt after a long day on the tennis courts.

Honestly, he does miss tennis, but he doesn't miss the country club. Part of his heart has always longed for the country, and he knows the other part of his heart longs for Gabby. He looks up to find the first star of the evening above, and his thoughts go to her. *Are you wishing on this same star? Come home; this is where you belong.*

The bellowing of the cattle is almost deafening. In his years away, he has forgotten. The calves cry for their mothers, and equally, the mothers call out loudly to their young. It makes him sad. He should have remembered to buy earplugs, because there will be little sleep tonight.

Brett hears some footsteps approaching, but he doesn't turn around. He can tell from listening to the stride that it is King. The ranch owner stands next to him. After a few seconds pass, King is the first to speak.

"You did a good job today," he says. He joins Brett by propping his own foot up on the fence rail.

Brett nods in acknowledgement, but he stays silent and continues to look straight ahead.

"I'm glad you're working here. I was a little surprised at first but happy nonetheless." He reaches into his belt, and he pulls out two flasks. "Here, I brought you some whiskey. You look like you could use a drink." King chuckles.

Brett glances over in the direction of the older cowboy and accepts the flask. "Thank you, sir."

"Rusty tells me that you're ready for the rodeo. He also says that you have been working hard and that your times are right where they should be." He pats Brett on the back. "I could see it the first time I saw you ride when you were just a young buck. It was a long time ago, but then after we rode that first time back in February, those memories all came back to me."

He's pleased that Rusty shared with King, but this is small talk. He wants to know about Gabby. He knows that King paid her a visit.

"How is she?" Brett asks as he looks out to the pastures.

"Well, we had a nice little chat. Motherhood looks good on her. By the way, she knows nothing about your letters—seems like they kind of got lost, if you get my drift. She can't figure out why she hasn't heard from you."

"I'm giving her some space. Isn't that what she wants?"

"Women are confusing. They want you to chase them, and when you do, they push you away. It's a game." King takes a swig from the flask.

Brett looks at him with a wrinkled brow. He is thankful for the burn of the whiskey in his throat, but it doesn't compare to the fire in his heart.

"What a racket," King says. "No one will get much sleep tonight. The whiskey will help. At least that's what I tell Rita." He takes a swig and wipes his mouth.

"The bond between a mother and her baby is the strongest, tightest bond on earth, stronger than the love between a man and a woman. I know that may be hard for you to accept, but it is true. Take some words of advice: if you want the heifer, you take the calf."

Brett tilts his head and stares at King with a furled brow.

"I promised my daughter that I wasn't going to meddle," King says, "but I also believe in fair play. So, here's one more thing—a warning; a vulture is circling." He winks and holds the flask up to his lips. "Sometimes, you just have to go and get what you want." He pats Brett on the shoulder. "For all of your hard work, you deserve a long weekend. Take the next few days off. Heck, take a week, however long it takes. Use the time well."

King pauses and then adds, "You may want to check out the Crystal Gallery website. It's some little place in Arlington, Virginia." He winks again before turning toward the house. Brett listens to the sound of King's boots on the gravel path until they fade away.

Brett leaves the ranch that evening and heads to town to pack for his trip. During the drive, he thinks about his conversation with King. He loves Gabby, and though he isn't ready to be a father, he isn't ready to lose Gabby. When is one ever ready to have a child? Sure, he would like to have a few years alone with her before adding a kid to the mix. Sure, he would like to have more money saved in the bank. But he recalls how his mother died in a car accident when he was only eight years old. Life is unpredictable, and it throws curve balls. Why did Gabby leave town? Did she think he wasn't capable of providing for a baby? Did she think he wouldn't be a good father?

Before going to his apartment, Brett has an idea. He pulls his car into a space at the jewelry store and walks inside.

"Mr. Matthews, how are you?" The jeweler looks up from the desk in the back of the store.

"Fine, fine," Brett answers. He twirls his car keys around his forefinger.

"What can I do for you? Did your lady friend like her earrings?"

"Yes, she loves them. That's why I'm here. Remember that bracelet, the one that matches the trinity knot earrings? Do you still have it?"

"Got it right here," the jeweler says. He stands and then opens the glass case and places the trinity knot bracelet on a black velvet cloth.

"That's the one." Brett picks up the bracelet and runs the chain through his fingers. "It's perfect. I'll take it."

As the jeweler is ringing up the sale, Brett checks out the display case with the engagement rings. *I don't know much about diamonds.* He looks up to find the jeweler smiling at him.

"I can help you with that." The man reaches under the glass and brings out one of the rings. "See this," he says. "It has a large stone. Some folks think that bigger is better." He gives Brett the magnifying glass. Then he says, "It has a few flaws, but no one will know."

The jeweler reaches under the case and brings out another ring with a smaller diamond. "Now, this one is a great stone…almost perfect. Check it out."

Once more, Brett looks through the magnifying glass. "Both rings are the same price." He knits his brow.

"Quality verses quantity. Congratulations," the jeweler says. Brett looks at the man with a puzzled stare.

"Finding the right gal is the hard part; finding the right ring is easy." He extends his hand. "Come back when you're ready."

Brett leaves the store with the box holding the bracelet. He thinks about the original meaning of the trinity knot that represented Gabby and her parents. However, this new trinity knot will represent their new family—Gabby, Brett, and their baby. He looks into his rear-view mirror and sees a man who is determined and confident. He likes this man, and he hopes that Gabby will like this man, too.

CHAPTER 19

Gabby

Where are we going?" Gabby asks. On this Saturday morning, the sun creates a patchy pattern on the field as the rays beam through the breaks in the layer of clouds. Stan drives the car down the narrow, winding road. They have been off the main freeway for the past ten minutes.

"It's a surprise. Believe me, you will love it," he says. "I don't know why I didn't think of it sooner."

"You're dressed for the ranch, but we aren't in Texas," she says.

"That's right. We're in Virginia. Virginia and Texas have a few things in common." He gives her a wink as he pulls the car through the open double gate that leads to a long drive for the Wild Berry Stables.

She sees the white, wooden fence bordering the road on both sides, and the animals grazing in the fields. She squeals in delight. "Horses!"

"You mentioned to me the other night that you missed the ranch.

Well, they call them farms and stables in this part of the country. My friend Eric works here. After you introduced me to riding, I came out here a few times to practice. I was keeping it a secret, but that's not necessary anymore."

She sits forward and watches as they arrive at the stable. Stan pulls his truck up to the barn and turns off the engine. He opens the door for her. A man walks toward them.

"Hi, Stan. Welcome," Eric says. Then he turns his attention to her. "You must be Gabby. Stan has told me a lot about you." He shakes her hand. "Welcome to Wild Berry Farm. I understand that you are in need of a horse fix. This is just the place." Eric is tall and lean with sandy blond hair. She likes that his handshake is firm.

"I got our horses saddled and ready to go," Eric says, looking at Stan. "But first, let's go meet Andrew. He can show Gabby around while we're out riding."

She catches Stan standing erect with his shoulders held back as if he were a proud peacock with a wide smile from ear to ear. She makes a face at him and he chuckles.

Eric takes the lead and walks to the stables, motioning them to follow. Gabby stops at each stall. "These horses are beautiful."

"We use them for our therapy sessions. I'm known as the horse-whisperer, and Andrew is the psychologist, AKA the people-whisperer. He runs the equine-assisted therapy program. I'll let him tell you more about that."

"I've read about that," she says.

"Hey, Andrew," Eric yells. "Stan and Gabby are here." They hear a voice answer from the far end of the barn. "From the direction of his voice, he must be working with Sadie. Come this way."

They walk the length of the building to the last stall. A large dark brown mare occupies the stall, and she is being brushed. Andrew, stocky and of medium height, has brown hair under a baseball cap, and a wide and contagious smile.

"I've heard so much about you," he says as he offers his hand to Gabby; however, he immediately pulls his hand back. "Sorry, I'm pretty dirty." He tips his cap back instead, "Nice to see you again, Stan." He pats Sadie on her side. "This is Sadie. She's a good ol' gal."

Gabby rubs Sadie's back and closes her eyes as she inhales the familiar scent of horses and hay, reminding her of her beloved Texas.

"We're going for a ride. It's been a while since Stan's ridden, so I want to make sure he hasn't forgotten everything I taught him. Do you mind keeping Gabby company?" Eric says to Andrew.

"That's not necessary," she says.

"You would be doing me a favor. It will give me fresh ears. Promise, that you'll stop me if I ramble on about the horse therapy," Andrew says. "I get so excited talking about the kids and how they have benefited from working with the horses."

Stan looks at her. "You okay with me leaving you with this guy?"

"I'll be fine. I want to hear more about the horse therapy, and I want to see you ride. I love being here. It is a wonderful treat."

"I think it's time we saddle up," Stan says to Eric.

Eric nods. "It's a perfect day. Let's go."

She looks on as Stan mounts a large black steed. *He has come a long way from the first time he went riding.* He waves to her, and she smiles back.

As Eric and Stan head off, Andrew takes Gabby on a tour of the farm. He also describes his work with the students. He explains that by teaching them how to work and communicate with the horse, he is indirectly teaching them how to deal with others.

"Some of the results are amazing. I have seen students with fear and anxiety issues improve sevenfold. Then we have a few patients who come here to ride because it helps them with their physical injuries. Riding helps strengthen muscle groups. Most patients think that riding is more fun than hanging out in the gym. Besides, the great outdoors can be the best therapy."

As they walk down the dirt path, Andrew stops and puts his hand up in the air. He points to a mare and her colt standing under the tree.

"See that little guy. He's just a week old. It's her first."

"He's so cute." It makes her think of her own baby, and she places her hand on her stomach.

They hear the hooves of the horses coming near, and they see Stan and Eric riding in the next field. Stan is galloping. "Impressive," she says to Andrew as she remembers Stan's first attempt at horseback riding. She smiles.

"He's worked hard," Andrew says. "He was obsessed with learning. We're surprised that we haven't seen him lately. I'm glad he stopped by."

"I believe I'm the one responsible for that. My moving here has distracted him."

In the car on the ride home from the farm, Gabby is absorbed in her thoughts. Stan is the first one to break the silence.

"Hey, you're quiet."

"I miss home," she says. "I miss Frog and Lady and Diesel..." *And Brett, but I can't say that to Stan.*

"Bringing you here was supposed to make you happy, but I see it has done just the opposite."

"No, it was a great day. Eric and Andrew are nice and very knowledgeable. I learned so much about the therapy program." She looks out the side window of the car. "I miss the ranch and our horses. I miss my friends. I miss tennis." She touches Stan's arm. "I don't mean to complain. I'm grateful for everything you have done. I know that once the baby is born, I can go back to doing some of those things."

"Speaking about friends, Will tells me that you and Ella have a shopping trip planned."

"Yes, even though I am not a fan of shopping, I am busting out of my clothes. I need to get a few in a larger size. Seeing Ella will perk me up, and she loves to shop, which will make my day far more enjoyable."

"Will and I can meet you ladies after work for dinner." He reaches over and squeezes her hand.

"Thanks—that would be nice." She looks out the window once again. Thank goodness for Ella. Ella is good at staying in contact with their tennis friends in Texas, and she loves to share their news. Gabby has purposely avoided her friends as she doesn't wish to answer questions and explain her whereabouts. Hearing about them from Ella may help to ease this homesickness.

Gabby's fingers go to her neck, and she indulges in her nervous habit once again. Thank God for her upcoming art show. That should keep her busy. *Maybe it's the hormones that are causing me to be moody.* Gabby knows that she is telling herself a lie. She misses Texas, and she misses Brett. Maybe she should take her daddy's advice and go home. As if on auto-pilot, her hand touches the trinity knot earrings, a gift from Brett. She shudders and rubs her arms as if to warm from the chill that has slowly creeped through her since she put distance between herself and the man that she loves. *What a tangled mess.*

CHAPTER 20

Gabby

W hat do you think?" Gabby asks Ella as she comes out of the dressing room and stands in front of the full-length mirror. The dress is dark-purple chiffon with a high waist and pleats down the front. Then she turns to the side and pulls the fabric tight around her middle. From the front view, the pleats hide her pregnancy. However, from the side, her pregnancy bump is clearly visible.

Ella covers her mouth. "It's absolutely perfect. The color suits your complexion. You look beautiful." She walks over to gather Gabby's blond hair and piles it on the top of her head. "Add the right pair of earrings, and you will be stunning. I love it." She gives Gabby a hug.

"Me too. Glad that chore is out of the way. You've been a big help today." Gabby wipes her brow as she slips off the dress and hangs it back on the hanger. The day proved successful; her shopping bags are full. This will be her last purchase. The art reception is just a few days away and she was in desperate need of a dress that fit her fast-growing figure.

Ella checks her phone. "We have an hour before meeting the boys, so let's get a drink, and you can prop your feet up."

"I would like that," Gabby looks down at her swollen ankles. Ella's phone rings, and she takes the call.

"Sorry, Gabby, but Will can't make dinner tonight. Something came up at the office, and he wants me to join him and his clients. You don't mind, do you?"

"No, of course not," Gabby says. "You go and have fun."

Her smile fades. She was looking forward to spending the evening with Will and Ella.

"Tell Stan hello from me, and we'll have to do dinner another evening soon, okay? Thanks for today," Ella says. After a brief kiss, she is gone.

The restaurant is dark and cozy. It's a small Italian place hidden on a side street in the heart of the city.

"I'm glad you liked your meal," Stan says as he glances over at her empty plate.

"I was starved. Shopping must have given me an appetite." She wipes her mouth with the corner of her napkin and smiles.

"I love your smile. It's nice to see you happy."

"You're right, I am happy. The baby is doing well. My art reception is in two days and I found the perfect dress. My daddy and your mother are coming to town. Life is good." She takes a sip of her water. Stan is leaning back in his chair smiling at her. "What?" she asks, but he remains silent. "And I owe you for helping me get my foot in the gallery door. Thank you."

"But it was your art that cinched the deal."

She takes his hand. "You are so good to me. I am so grateful. The list is long. You gave me, I mean us, a place to live. You encourage my art." She gazes at him. "You cook, you clean, you rub my feet. You have been a great friend."

"You don't get it, do you?"

She tries to pull her hand away, but he holds on even more tightly. "Get what?" she asks, looking into his earnest brown eyes.

"Us. Look at us, Gabby. We're good together … real good together." She lowers her eyes. "We're happy. We don't fight." He squeezes her hand. "I love you, Gabby. I've loved you from the first moment I met you."

"But—"

"Just hear me out. I've waited. I let you sort your life out. You haven't gone back to Richard."

"Heavens, no."

"You haven't gone back to Brett."

She shifts her weight in her chair, unable to look at him.

"If Brett loved you, Gabby, really loved you, nothing would keep him away. Think about it. A lot of time has passed."

This time, she succeeds in pulling her hand away. She turns away and bites her lip.

"I'm just stating the obvious. I don't mean to upset you." He reaches for her hand again. His touch is warm and strong. She feels his calluses from the long days working at the motorcycle shop.

"I love you. I'll love the baby. Pick me, Gabby. Pick us. Your baby deserves a father. I can be that. We can do this together. We make the perfect family."

Tears form in her eyes. *Why hasn't Brett tried to call? Stan is right. If Brett loved me, he would have tracked me down.*

Stan's voice gets louder. "If you miss Texas, hell, I'll move. I already learned to ride and I'll even buy a gun. I'll do whatever it takes."

Gabby laughs and wipes the tear that is rolling down her cheek. "The snakes better be on guard," she manages to say.

"Nothing would make me happier," he pats her hand. "I'm in my mid-thirties. I'd love to settle down and have a family. Please don't cry." He hands her a napkin to dab her eyes.

"You have been such a kind, kind soul. I'm forever grateful."

"Think about it, my love." He leans over and brushes her lips with a soft kiss. "I know that I can make you happy."

Stan sits back. His plea has been delivered. She catches another tear with the napkin, sniffles, before forcing a weak smile. Could she make a life with Stan?

CHAPTER 21

Gabby

H ello," Gabby calls as she enters the gallery. The bells jingle, and the door closes behind her.

"I'll be with you in a minute," Janet yells from the back room.

The gallery is quiet and empty. In awe, she stands and stares at the blank white walls. She recalls a cozy, friendly atmosphere when she first visited three weeks ago. However, today the gallery looks so much bigger and intimidating. A sense of doubt overtakes her, and she feels small in comparison. Why is she behaving like this is her first exhibit?

She should be feeling excited. This is her debut art show in Virginia. Deep in thought, she doesn't hear Janet's footsteps.

"Gabby, are you all right?" Janet asks. "It's as if you are a million miles away."

"Sorry, I was just thinking. Planning, really, trying to figure out which paintings would look better where."

"It will all come together," Janet says. "Sometimes, the paintings speak for themselves, and they tell you where they want to hang."

Gabby grins. Janet has a way of making her feel at ease.

Janet says, "Hanging a new show is my favorite part of this job. Giving a voice to fresh, creative works so they can speak is a thrill like none other."

Her enthusiasm makes the tension leave Gabby's body. She takes a deep breath and stands straighter as if a big weight has been lifted from her shoulders.

After unloading the canvases from Stan's truck, the women break for lunch. Gabby stands on the steps and inhales deeply as Janet displays the Closed sign and locks the gallery door.

"Hanging goes so much better on a full stomach," Janet says as she ushers Gabby down the street to a tiny outdoor café. Under a partly cloudy sky, the temperatures are mild. Walking to the café helps clear her head. Janet's open and friendly attitude puts her more at ease.

At lunch, Janet asks, "Have you thought about making prints of your artwork?"

Gabby stops chewing and glances up.

"I'm asking because if one of the decorators likes your work, he will want prints, not just the original." Janet puts her fork down on the plate. "I know that artists feel conflicted, and there is much discussion in the art world about original works versus prints. Some think large numbers in print cheapens their work. Others are happy that their work was chosen for mass production. I'm mentioning it so that you can think about it, and when the topic comes up at the reception, it's not a surprise."

Gabby thinks about her baby and her desire to make a living. She wants to be independent even though she is the rich Wayne King's only heir. "If there's an interest, I will consider marketing my abstracts as prints, but I wish to keep my knot collections as original fine art."

"I can live with that decision," Janet says. "If you change your mind, let me know."

After lunch, back at the gallery, the women work all afternoon. They group the Zeppelin Bend Knot collection together and spread the pastel abstract works on the other two walls.

"There, done. See, that went smoothly," Janet says. "What do you think?"

Gabby looks up at the walls dressed in her familiar art. The coldness that she sensed earlier is gone. "It's perfect," she says.

"Well, it's not perfect, yet. I'll get out the level and make sure it is perfect, but I wanted your okay that the pieces are hanging as you wish. We can move some around. Take your time. I'll make us some tea."

Gabby sits on a chair as Janet disappears into the back room.

Gabby glances up at her Zeppelin Bend paintings. The diptych catches her eye. She had initially hung the two paintings with space between them. Once she had thought the painting with half of the knot had a strong enough composition to stand by itself; however, after hanging it on the large white wall, it seemed lost, and it begged for its mate. Two months ago, she was so sure that it could stand alone, but after trying to hang them apart, she was overcome with doubt. Now, they hang ever so close. At a glance, a viewer could mistake them for a single canvas. Why the change? Has she made the wrong decision about raising her baby as a single mother?

She recalls the joy she felt after completing her first in the Zeppelin Bend series, "New Beginnings," the painting she gave to Rita and her daddy the night before their wedding. She was filled with hope for the joining of their two families. Studying the knot, she wonders if she and Stan should be together as well.

PART III

CHAPTER 22

Gabby

Gabby looks in the mirror as she puts on her trinity knot earrings to complete her outfit. She has put her hair up in a loose twist with soft curls hanging down as Ella had suggested. The purple dress flows softly as she moves her hips back and forth. She turns to the side. Her pregnancy bump is noticeable. It has been almost two months since she came to Washington. It is early July, near the end of her second trimester, and she has gained fifteen pounds. Her doctor tells her that everything is going well, and Stan frequently tells her that she is beautiful.

She remembers her last art exhibition at Rita's gallery in Texas. It was a January afternoon when these earrings arrived on her doorstep. They were a gift from Brett, and she has worn them almost every day since. She looks down at her puffy ankles and kicks off her four-inch spiked heels. It was silly for her to consider wearing them. She closes her eyes, recalling how Brett massaged her aching feet after that exhibition, and it was that night that they shared their first kiss. She remembers the stirrings of desire and the undeniable chemistry. How far would they have gone if Richard hadn't returned to the gallery?

If the doctor's calculations are right, it was that night after their argument, when Richard claimed her in a jealous rage. If she had pushed him away, she wouldn't be in her present-day predicament. Gabby bites her lip and rubs her stomach again.

Brett

Brett watches the gallery entrance from the small restaurant across the street. He had eaten lunch there earlier, and now he sits at a bar table by the window. He has been watching and waiting. A couple exits a yellow cab; the man gets out first and then he holds the door and helps the woman. Her blond hair catches his eye first. As the taxi pulls away, he knows that it is her.

The man puts his arm around her, and Brett takes a sip of his whiskey. He wasn't going to drink, but the longer he has waited, the more anxious he has become, and he needs something to quiet his nerves. He sees the couple smiling, and his heart drops. *Did I expect her to be sad? To have missed me so much that she would eagerly welcome me back into her arms? Maybe this was a bad idea, and I should get on the next plane back to Texas.*

He is reminded of King's words: a vulture is circling. *Is Stan the vulture?* He taps his fingers on the glass.

Of course, he knew that Will and Stan lived in D.C. But he had envisioned Gabby living with Ella. He should have come earlier. Maybe Gabby is with Stan. Brett's intuition was right from the start. He had sensed that Stan was trouble at King's wedding. He bangs his fist on the table. The motion causes the whiskey to slide up the sides of the glass and spill over the edge, so he puts his glass down and shakes his head.

Brett sees her turn to walk up the steps. The reality of her pregnancy causes him to suck in his breath. Even though he tried to prepare for this moment, it still comes as a shock to him. His pulse races and his stomach drops.

"I thought that was you."

Brett turns toward the voice.

"So, the cowboy left Texas," Ella says. "Does Gabby know you're in town?" She pauses, and then continues, "Of course, she doesn't. I just talked with her, and your name never came up in the conversation."

Ella and Will are standing arm-in-arm next to his table.

"Hello, Will," Brett says as he nods his head. Not waiting for any small talk, Brett says, "Richard told me that Gabby's pregnant. I guess I had to see it for myself."

"Why would Richard tell you?" Ella asks as she crosses her arms over her chest.

"He thought I should know."

Ella cocks her head to the side and then her eyes light up. "Oh, I get it. It's his kid. He has bragging rights." She giggles.

Brett's face pales, and his mouth drops open. *It's Richard's kid. No wonder Gabby is acting so strange. It is all making sense. I can always count on you, Ella.*

"Oh my God, you didn't know," she stammers. She covers her mouth with her hands.

Brett stays silent and observes Will rolling his eyes. It must be true. His heart sinks in the silence that follows. His face remains as white as a sheet. Gathering the strength to regain his composure, he forces a smile and says, "Ella, you look great. Washington must agree with you."

"Washington is great. I really love living in the city. You haven't heard our good news." She pulls Will in closer. "Will and I are engaged." She sticks out her left hand and flashes her large diamond ring in Brett's face. "Will proposed last night. He's made me the happiest woman ever." She snuggles up to Will and puts her arm around his waist.

Brett lifts his whiskey glass, glad for the change in conversation. "Congratulations to both of you. When is the wedding?"

"Soon, real soon," Ella says. "We don't want to wait." She and Will look at each other.

"I'm happy for you." Brett lowers his eyes and focuses on his drink. Watching the happy couple is too much for his soul to bear.

"Ella, we should go." Will motions toward the door.

"I guess we'll see you later. Gabby will be surprised," she says. Brett sees her mouth twitch as she forces a smile before turning and going out the door. He watches as they cross the street arm in arm.

He sits alone at the table and looks out the window toward the gallery. He has been a fool. He thought that he was the father. He thought that Gabby didn't want to commit to their relationship because she wasn't ready. Now he knows that none of those things are true. He recalls King's words: "If you want the heifer, you take the calf."

He swirls the whiskey around in his glass. All of the planned speeches that he has rehearsed numerous times in his head are flawed. They were speeches about their child, his and Gabby's child, not Richard's. He orders another round. He needs to think.

He tries to recall the details of the image of Stan and Gabby as they walked into the gallery. They looked so happy together. Are they a couple? *How can Stan be so happy when he knows that he isn't the father of Gabby's baby? Can I swallow my pride? Should I leave and go home? I'm not wanted here. Gabby has made her choice. But if I leave, can I live with my choice? Should I tell her I love her?*

Gabby

At the gallery, Stan opens the door for Gabby. Their eyes meet and he says, "You look lovely tonight. I'm proud to be your escort."

"You look wonderful yourself. I'm so used to seeing you in your motorcycle attire. You clean up pretty well." She giggles. "And tonight there's only a hint of the smell of grease."

Stan shakes his head.

Gabby searches the gallery, making an inventory of her paintings, and checks to see if they are hanging level. On the table, she finds several dozen pink roses in a clear vase. She walks over to them, touches their soft petals, and leans in to smell them. The aroma brings back fond memories of holidays and special occasions. She knows who sent them without looking at the card, but she opens it anyway and grins. *He is so thoughtful.* Her father has never missed sending pink roses for one of her art receptions.

Janet comes out of the back room carrying some glasses. "I'm glad you're here early." She puts the tray of wine glasses on the table. "Hey, Stan, can you open these bottles of wine and put them on ice?"

"What can I do to help?" Gabby asks.

"Sit and relax while you can. You will be on your feet for the next few hours." Janet motions to a row of chairs. "We got this. I just need to bring out the cheese platter, and we are good to go." She looks at her watch. "With ten minutes to spare." She gives Gabby a hug. "I'm looking forward to meeting the rest of your family. You look as pretty as one of your paintings. The pink roses are a nice touch. One would think you were having a girl."

Gabby doesn't respond even though she sees Stan look from her to Janet, waiting.

"Several of the decorators are coming from that interior design company down the street. I got their RSVP this morning. Have you given thought to our conversation about making prints of your entire collection?" Janet asks. "Have you changed your mind?"

"No, but I could be persuaded. Let's see if there is an interest, then I can give you a definite answer."

Gabby pretends that she is a viewer looking at the art on the walls for the first time. What would her impression be? The bells jingling on the gallery door interrupt her thoughts. Her daddy and Rita have arrived.

"Hello, kitten." King makes his way over to where she is standing.

"Hi, Daddy. Thank you for the flowers. You're so thoughtful." She gives her daddy a quick hug and then steps back.

"Stan," King says, shaking his hand.

Rita gives Gabby a hug. "I've missed you and my dear sweet boy so much." Rita hugs Stan.

"Me too, I'm so glad you're here." She turns to face Janet. "This is Rita."

"Hello, Rita, it's so nice to meet you. Gabby speaks very highly of you. Later, we'll have to chat about running a gallery. Do a little networking," Janet says. "It's wonderful that Gabby is surrounded by family tonight. We hope to have a full house."

"We're very proud of Gabby. We wouldn't miss it," King puffs out his chest and removes his Stetson as he nods his head toward his daughter.

Gabby watches as Rita slowly makes her rounds of the gallery. Rita stops at the wall where the Zeppelin Bend paintings hang. Stan is next to his mother, and they seem to be in deep conversation.

"Do you have a favorite?" Gabby asks Rita as she joins them.

Rita answers, "The diptych is interesting. Notice how the two sides mirror each other. It's clever to spread the knot over two canvases. When you gave us 'New Beginnings,' you said that it represented the union of our two families. With the knot spread over two canvases, I see each family still has its core even though it is in close proximity to the other."

"That's an interesting interpretation," Gabby says, trying to see her painting with new eyes. "I like it." *Maybe Stan and I should be a couple.*

Brett

Brett has difficulty concentrating with the startling news Ella accidentally revealed. It takes another full shot of whiskey to talk himself out of calling a cab and heading back to the airport. He takes his time digesting the information and formulating a new plan before approaching Gabby at the art gallery.

Now, he's prepared. After paying his bar bill, he straightens his clothing. He holds his head up high as he crosses the street to the gallery. He has watched at least a dozen cars pull up out front and has seen at least another dozen people walking from the direction of the Metro. There will be a crowd so it will be hard to get Gabby alone, but he must get her attention.

Inhaling deeply, he opens the art gallery door.

Immediately, Stan blocks the entrance with his arm. "You're not invited."

Brett knocks his arm away and pushes past. "Open to the public. Guess I'm invited."

"It's best that you leave. I don't want Gabby upset."

Stan gets close to him and blocks his path once more.

"Why don't we ask Gabby what she wants?" Brett says. He grabs Stan by the lapel of his suit jacket. "Does Gabby know you've been deceiving her…keeping things from her? You have had your own agenda, mister, and it's going to stop. Who appointed you her guardian angel?"

Stan grabs his wrist and squeezes hard. "You haven't been around. If you cared so much, you would have been there for her when she needed you. She's better off without you."

Brett stands firm. "And let me guess, you think you're what she needs, you lying SOB. You purposely kept us apart. I should deck you right here."

Will steps between them. "As much as I would enjoy watching this showdown, this is not the place."

Will places his hand on his brother's shoulder. "You don't want to embarrass yourself in front of our friends and Gabby." Then Will looks to Brett. "It would be best for you to leave."

Reluctantly, Stan releases his grip on Brett's wrist. Brett steps back. "I didn't come here to cause trouble. If she has picked you, you have nothing to worry about." He looks back and forth from Stan to Will. "I need to hear it from Gabby."

Stan says, "You chose tonight of all nights to talk to her—poor choice, buddy, not the right time."

"Would you rather I talk with her later? Alone?" He chuckles. "Didn't think so."

Brett pushes by Stan and finds Gabby in the back of the gallery speaking with her dad. Ella and Rita are close by. He sees King glance in his direction and then nod in approval. Grateful to have someone in his corner, he stands next to King.

He and Gabby lock eyes. Her eyes are wide, and she appears flustered. Time stands still. He waits for her to speak first. Likewise, she waits for him to speak. The silence is awkward.

"Brett," she says. "Wh-what a surprise! I didn't expect to see you here."

They are interrupted by the sound of glass. From the other side of the room, Janet taps a wine glass with a spoon.

When the room quiets, Janet says, "Thank you for coming tonight. I am pleased to introduce our featured artist, Miss Gabriella King. She has exhibited in Houston, Dallas, Austin, and New York City and now here at the Crystal Gallery. Please give her a warm welcome."

He watches as she walks to the front of the room and stands next to Janet. He is mesmerized. She is so beautiful. At times during these past few months, he had secretly hoped that his feelings for her would fade. But now, after seeing her again, he knows that he loves her more than he thought possible. Nothing has changed for him. Her voice is sweet music to his ears. Her face has infiltrated his every waking moment. His pulse racing, he needs to talk to her and hold her. Surely, she'll remember their shared chemistry, how her breathing quickens under his touch. They need to talk before the night is over. Janet's timing is impeccable at keeping them apart again. He's not going anywhere. He'll wait a lifetime for her it that's what it will take.

She glows in the spotlight. There are so many people between her and where he is standing. Slowly, he makes his way toward her, advancing through the guests, begging for her to look in his direction. He gets closer and closer.

She addresses the crowd. "Thank you for coming tonight. Your support means so much. I want to thank Janet and the Crystal Gallery for thinking my art worthy."

His eyes follow her arm as she extends it. Instantaneously her eyes meet his. Their eyes lock. "Here's to all of you." Gabby lifts her glass in the air. He sees her sway and then—

He hastens his steps. He must reach her.

Gabby

Brett steps forward and catches her a split-second before her head reaches the floor. He holds her with her head cradled in her arms. The crowd gasps. Instantly, Janet clears the area around them.

"Give her some air," Janet motions for all to step back, then starts fanning Gabby with a booklet.

Gabby's eyes open. "What happened?" She thinks she is dreaming as she focuses on his familiar face. This same face has filled her dreams at night and has taken over her thoughts during the day. She would be content if time stopped at this very moment.

Their moment is interrupted by Janet. "Gabby, talk to me. You fainted. Are you having any pain or bleeding?"

"I don't think so," Gabby answers softly. "I got light-headed, and then everything went black." She keeps gazing into his familiar emerald green eyes, and reaching deeply she finds a piece of her soul. The flutter in her chest is confirmation of her love.

Brett

In the meantime, Stan has pushed his way through the guests to get to Gabby. He stands over her and says, "I'm taking you to the hospital." He then turns to Brett. "Look what you've done. I told you to go away."

"I'm not going anywhere. If Gabby asks me to leave, then I'll leave," Brett says sternly.

She says, "Stan, please."

Stan continues on his rampage. "We don't need him here."

"It's okay. I want him here," she says. King pats Stan on the shoulder and ushers him away to where Rita and Will are standing.

"We're lucky that this man was here to catch your fall," Janet says. She looks at Brett, who is still holding Gabby's head on his lap. "We haven't had the pleasure. Hi, I'm Janet."

"I'm Brett. Pleasure to meet you, ma'am."

Janet takes Gabby's pulse and notes that it is strong, even, and her skin is warm and dry. "I was a nurse before I opened the gallery." She holds Gabby's wrist. "Your vitals are fine, and since you aren't in any pain, I think you fainted. Pregnant women do that sometimes.

But you should make an appointment with your doctor to be sure everything is okay."

Brett whispers, "I'll always be here for you, Gabby. That is, if you want me." He smells her familiar perfume, and he can't help but caress her soft skin. He could stay right here forever. Being with Gabby is the fulfillment of his deepest desire. It is a scene that he has envisioned in his dreams more times than he can count. "I'm not letting you go this time."

Janet leans toward them and whispers, "I really hate to interrupt, but we have guests. Gabby, are you ready to try standing? I think our guests need to see that you're okay."

"I think I can," Gabby says with a determined look on her face. Brett helps her to her feet and steadies her with his arm around her waist. Someone watching could mistake his hold as being for her safety, but he can't release her. Now that he has found her, he'll hold on tight, not wanting to be alone ever again.

The rest of the evening progresses without incident. Gabby assures her guests that she is all right, and she speaks about her art with them in small groups or in one-on-one conversations. Brett steals nervous glances her way as he views the artwork. He is anxious to get her alone, but he realizes that this is her evening; he will have to wait. Also conscious of Stan and Will, he avoids standing near them because he doesn't want another confrontation. Stan has been in control long enough, and that is ending tonight. Brett is not leaving. That just isn't an option. He has waited months to get his time with Gabby, and he can wait another few hours.

Meanwhile, as Gabby is occupied speaking to the guests, Brett scans the artwork on the walls. These abstract paintings are different from any of her previous works. Usually she works in vibrant color; instead, these are dominantly pastels, giving them a soft quality. He wonders if motherhood has anything to do with the change.

Continuing to view the artwork, he feels someone standing next to him.

King says, "I can't thank you enough for catching her."

"I could sense that something wasn't right. Call it instinct," Brett says. "I just knew I had to get there."

"I've always known that you're fast, but that was still incredible. That's why you're my pick at the rodeo next week. Anyway, we can talk about the rodeo another time. I'm glad you're here tonight."

He confirms what King stated. "Yes, it is good that I'm here. Sometimes you have to go and get what you want."

"Indeed you do." King lifts his glass and gives Brett's glass a solid click.

Gabby

As the evening winds down, Gabby stands at the door and thanks each guest for attending. As Will and Ella approach, Gabby asks, "Where is Stan?"

Will answers, "His pride is injured. He left an hour ago. Can we give you a ride?"

"No, thanks. I can get a ride with Daddy or take a cab."

Ella nods in Brett's direction.

"I know I owe him an explanation. I've really made a mess of things," Gabby says.

191

"I'm sorry," Ella says. "I may have said something earlier to Brett that I shouldn't have said."

"You have nothing to be sorry about. I did this myself." She reaches for her necklace. "I didn't handle any of this properly. I'm sort of relieved that everything will soon be out in the open."

"I'm sorry you're having to deal with this whole mess. Hope you start feeling better. Call me tomorrow after you see your doctor. Promise?" Ella gives her a hug and leaves.

Gabby turns her attention to the remaining guests: Daddy, Rita, and Brett. They are talking and laughing with Janet. She looks at Brett's profile. He is different from when she left Texas. He seems more grounded, giving him an appearance of maturity and confidence. She hears their laughter. She's thrilled that her daddy and Brett are friends. She can tell by the way her daddy stands close to Brett when they are engaged in a conversation that they share a mutual bond and respect.

Suddenly, thoughts of Stan pop into her mind. Stan must be terribly upset for him to leave without any explanation. Gabby sighs and bites her upper lip. Stan has been by her side, and she has allowed him to care for her. He has professed his love for her on several occasions. It is true that she has never reciprocated his advances. However, she hasn't discouraged him either. He is a good person. He will make someone a great husband and father. *But that someone isn't me.*

She has told him on several occasions that she is grateful for everything he has done, but gratitude is not love. Stan doesn't cause her to swoon when he comes near. Stan doesn't cause her heart to race when she looks into his eyes.

Brett seems to sense Gabby staring, and he walks toward her. "Are you feeling better?"

"Yes, I'm okay. I don't know what happened." She looks down to avoid looking at his concerned face. Her heart races. *Damn, why does he do this to me?* "Thank you for catching me."

"Gabby, we need to talk. Why didn't you call me, text me, or answer my letters? Everyone told me not to pressure you and to give you time. I couldn't wait any longer. God, I've missed you."

She relishes the warm touch of his hand as he turns her to face him so that their eyes meet.

"I thought we had something special. If you love someone, you talk to them. You don't run away."

He touches her again, and her breathing quickens. Every part of her wants to reach out to him, touch him, and caress him. She needs him.

Reason takes over. "I can't do this. Not here. Please," she begs. Her voice cracks, but she must pretend to be strong and forces back her tears.

"You hurt me, Gabby. Really hurt me. Why would you do that? There is so much that I don't understand."

She closes her eyes and hangs her head. "I'm so sorry. We can't talk here. It is so complicated. I would never purposely hurt you." She reaches for his hand. "You must believe me. There is so much you don't know."

"You chose for it to be this way, Gabby. Look at you! You're pregnant. Did you think I wouldn't find out? Did you ever put yourself in my shoes?"

"Keep your voice down." She looks around to see if her daddy and Rita are listening. "I had decisions to make, lots of them. Like I said before, it's complicated. I'm sorry that I hurt you."

"Sorry that you hurt me. We're way past sorry, Gabby. You owe me an explanation. Why do you think you have the right to make all of these decisions on your own? Why can't we make them together? If you don't want me, then tell me. You can tell me right now, and I'll walk away." He shifts his weight.

Her heart flutters. She doesn't want him to walk away. Can't he tell how much she loves him? She needs to give him something. From reading his eyes and hearing his words, she is hurting him again. She wants to end the pain. Why can't she tell him she loves him? What is holding her back?

"Most men would have been long gone by now. You realize that, right?"

Gabby closes her eyes and is unable to face him. He's right. Most men would be gone. She needs to use her voice. She needs to tell him that he is not the father of the life she carries. Her acts of omission are the reason for her silence. She can't tell him what he wants to hear. Her declaration of love would seem insincere until she divulges that Richard is the father of her unborn child. What can she say to reassure him to stick around?

"I know I owe you some answers. I should have told you months ago." She glances over at her dad, Rita, and Janet. "I can't talk with you tonight. I need to wrap things up here. You know, thank Janet for everything." Her voice quivers. "Come back here tomorrow, and we'll talk. We'll talk for hours, if you want. I don't have the strength to talk tonight. Please, can we have this conversation tomorrow?" Her eyes are pleading. "It's been a really long day."

"You want me to leave?" His eyes are wide, and his mouth hangs open. "I come here to see you, pour out my heart to you, and you want me to leave?" He shakes his head and looks down at his feet.

"Yes…but we'll talk tomorrow." She reaches over and strokes his arm. She needs to give him something to hold on to. She doesn't want him out of her life. "Tomorrow, I promise."

Brett sets his jaw. This is not what he expected.

"It's really good to see you. I'm glad you are here." She gets up on her toes and brushes his cheek with her lips. "I've missed you," she whispers in his ear.

He holds her face in his hands and shakes his head. "You're killing me," he says. "Do you know that?"

She has missed that dimple, and she smiles to reassure him that there is a chance for them to be together. "I'll see you tomorrow?"

"Yeah, tomorrow." He backs away and walks out the door into the night.

She watches him disappear into the darkness, and her heart cries to follow him. She is turning to speak with Janet when she hears the bells on the door jingle, causing her to turn around.

"Did you forget something?" she asks. *Why has he returned?*

"Yeah, this." Brett stands close to her and pulls her in tightly. "Do you really expect me to walk away? Do you really want me to leave?"

She smells his spicy scent and feels his heart beating fast and hard. He turns his head and lifts her chin. She doesn't look away. His lips are soft and his kiss gentle. Why did she think she could forget? All of their shared memories come flooding back. Her body melts into his. She is greedy for his lips and feels light-headed again, which causes her to lean more closely into his body. She has missed his kiss, his embrace; she has missed everything about him.

After they separate, he says, "A wise cowboy told me that if I wanted something, I needed to go after it." He winks at her and then he reaches into his pocket. "Here, I forgot to give you this. I got you a present." He hands her the box from the jewelry store.

She can't stop her hand from shaking, and she is aware that he can see her rapid breathing. "A wise cowboy." She looks in her daddy's direction.

"You can open it later." He grins and flashes his dimple. "Tomorrow." He turns and exits into the night once again.

Gabby stands staring at the door, a part of her hoping that he will return again. She has tried to forget. These past two months she has distanced herself. She even tried convincing herself that she could love Stan. However, there is no denying true love. The box she is holding is shaking, but she cannot steady her hand, so she puts it away in her purse. She will open it later when she is alone. Her daddy makes his way to her.

King says, "You okay? I gather the two of you have resolved some issues from what I just witnessed." He winks.

Gabby looks him in the eye. "Why do I get the feeling that you had something to do with Brett coming here tonight?"

"Oh, I may have mentioned your show. However, Brett didn't tell me he was coming. When are you going to sit down and level with him?" King glances up at Rita before he continues. "Stan is pretty smitten with you as well. Rita is concerned."

"I've made a mess of everything. There are so many loose ends. I need to speak with Stan and with Brett."

"From what I saw tonight, you've made your choice." King clears his throat. "And I think Stan knows as well." King looks over to Rita and Janet. "I'm going to get my lovely bride and then we'll give you a ride home."

She watches her dad walk away. She grabs for her necklace and swings the trinity knot back and forth on its chain. She is reminded of her Zeppelin Bend series, and she studies the paintings on the wall. By involving members of both families, instead of finding clarity, she has made a bigger mess of her situation. Can she untangle the knot she created?

Gabby bids farewell to her daddy, Rita, and Janet, and she arrives at the condo and digs in her purse for the key. Unlocking the door, she stands in the dark. She will be quiet as not to wake Stan. Carefully, she removes her shoes and tiptoes across the living room to her bedroom.

As she passes through to the hall, a voice says, "I saw you with him. I was waiting outside the gallery. I didn't want you to come home alone."

She reaches to turn on the light.

"I'd rather sit in the dark," Stan says from the living room.

"Okay," she says, then hesitates. "Can I join you?" She carefully makes her way to the couch.

"If you wish. But I'll warn you that I won't be very good company. With that out of the way, how are you?" His tone is cold.

"I'm tired." She settles into the couch and props her feet up. "The reception went well, except for—" She rubs her stomach. "I can't believe I fainted."

"You need to take better care of yourself. But you're not my concern anymore. I've been sitting here, trying to face reality. It sucks, by the way." He pulls his feet down off the coffee table. "I'm surprised that you're here. I thought you would be with him."

"Stan—"

"No, let me finish. I saw you with him. All of these weeks that we spent together, they were good weeks, right? We laughed. We danced. I thought you and I had something special."

He puts the bottle on the coffee table. "Do you realize how many times I've wanted you to kiss me like that?"

Now, she is the one who is glad for the darkness. It matches the conversation that she has been dreading. "I looked for you at the gallery, but Ella and Will told me that you left."

"As I said, I was waiting outside. I saw the way he looks at you. But more importantly, I saw the way you look at him." He lifts the beer and takes a swig. "You don't look at me that way. I tried to make you forget about him. I thought maybe, just maybe I would have a chance. But after tonight it's crystal clear that I have been a fool to think that we could have a future together." He puts the bottle on the coffee table and gets up.

"Stan, please—"

"I'm going to bed." He gestures toward the kitchen. "There's some mail for you on the table."

"I don't understand."

"You will," he says as he walks down the hallway. "I'm sorry." His voice is quiet, sullen. He closes his bedroom door.

She walks to the kitchen and turns on the light. Beaming back at her on the table are several white envelopes. Immediately, she recognizes Jamie's handwriting. "Oh, dear," she whispers quietly. She looks at the postage cancellation marks. One of them was mailed shortly after she arrived. Has Stan been keeping them all this time?

I thought Brett wasn't interested, that he didn't care. She recalls Stan's words. *Surely, if he cared, he would have contacted you.* Stan has been lying to her. She holds the letters close to her heart. She doesn't need to open them. She knows what they will say. She remembers the box and takes it out of her purse. Should she open it?

These must be the letters Rita and her daddy were referring to when they asked her why she never responded. After so much time has passed, she will wait to open them after she speaks with Brett tomorrow. She puts the box back in her purse. This too, should wait until she and Brett have a chance to talk tomorrow.

Gabby undresses, removes the clip, and her hair cascades down her back. Her mood is lighter. Sitting at her vanity, she pulls the brush through her hair and becomes aware that she is humming. Thinking about Brett makes her hungry for his touch. The scent of spice lingers on her skin. Her appetite of desire has been awakened. She glances at the clock. Can she wait until noon tomorrow?

Nestled under the covers, the stars on her ceiling glow back at her, and she is reminded once more of her mother's words. Gabby makes a wish.

CHAPTER 23

Gabby

Gabby glances at her cellphone. It is half past noon. She thought Brett would be here by now. Where is he? Maybe he has changed his mind. Janet looks up and shakes her head. The older woman smiles.

"He'll be here. Nothing can keep him away," Janet says from behind her desk at the gallery.

Gabby looks at her, with her mouth open.

"I saw the way he looks at you. You're a lucky girl, having two men fight over you. Mercy, mercy," Janet says as she puts her hand on her chin. "It was quite a show."

"I'm sorry, Janet. I had no idea that Brett would come to the reception."

"No, no, dear. There's no need to apologize. It is the most excitement we've had around here in a while." She giggles. "So romantic. I wouldn't have missed it."

"Janet, stop it. He's coming. Okay." Gabby wrings her hands.

The bells on the door jingle, and Brett walks through with a bouquet of flowers. Gabby receives a quick kiss on the lips, then he walks past her to Janet.

"These are for you, pretty lady," he says and hands her the bouquet.

"What a surprise. You already have my vote, but the flowers are a nice touch," Janet says, smiling.

Brett turns back to face Gabby. "You ready for lunch? How long do we have?"

"I'm finished here. Janet was nice enough to give me the rest of the day off."

Looking over her glasses at Brett, Janet says, "See, I told you that you had my vote." She waves her hands as if shooing them out the door. "Now, you both run along. Have fun."

Gabby grabs her purse, and Brett wraps his arm around her. "You heard the woman, let's go."

"Bye, Janet. Thank you," she says as she and Brett go out the door.

Once outside, Brett leans up against the stone wall. He pulls her in close for a lavish kiss.

"I thought of nothing but you all night," he says as he backs away. "How do hot dogs in the park sound to you?" he asks as he nuzzles close to her ear.

"Really, that's a surprise," she says. "I'd like that. I miss wide-open spaces."

They walk hand in hand underneath a clear blue sky to the park, only a block away from the main street. At the tree-lined entrance, kids are playing around a water fountain. They stand and watch before moving on. He sees her touch her stomach.

He purchases the hot dogs and a bag of popcorn. They find a bench and sit. After finishing their lunch, they both start to speak at once.

"No, me first," She places her forefinger on his lips. She reaches into her purse. She brings out his letters that remain unopened and the box that he gave her the night before.

"What is this?" Brett asks. His eyes are wide.

"I never got your letters. Stan gave them to me last night. It seems he was trying to keep us apart." She lifts the envelopes for Brett to see. "I haven't opened them. So much time has passed since you wrote them. I know that time changes things. I didn't want to read them and then find out that your feelings have changed."

He takes the letters from her hand. "It does seem like a lifetime ago. You're right, lots of things have changed."

She pinches her lips together and looks down at her lap.

He reaches over and uses his forefinger to lift up her chin. "Don't be sad. Let me explain. A few weeks after you left, I quit my job at the country club. Now, I'm working for your dad."

"Yes, Rita told me."

"Richard came into the club and made the grand announcement that you were pregnant. For the past few weeks, I thought I was the father. I had this whole speech rehearsed about you, me, and our baby. But now my speech is irrelevant because yesterday, I learned that Richard is the father." Brett cocks his head to the side. "Gabby, do you have any idea of the turmoil you put me through? You need to level with me, right now. What is the truth?"

"You have every right to be upset. I was confused. I was scared that I would lose you."

"Well, pretending that I didn't exist is a good sure way to lose me."

She pinches her lip again.

"I wish you would have talked to me, you know, confided in me."

"It's a long story." She twists her hands together and looks across the grass at the kids playing.

He takes her hands in his. "Start talking. Take all the time you need. I need to understand."

"I didn't know I was pregnant until after Daddy's wedding. I visited the doctor and when he gave me the due date, I knew that you weren't the father. I loved you so much, I didn't want to lose you. My first thought was to go to Houston, get an abortion, and no one would be the wiser. But I couldn't do it. I was scared and needed time to think. You were pressuring me to move in together, and I was feeling the pressure of being pregnant. I didn't think you would want to be saddled down with a child, especially when it isn't even yours."

"Don't you think you should have asked?"

"It was a very difficult time. In hindsight, I should have told you. Daddy begged me to tell you, but I was frightened. I needed time, so I came here. The plan was for me to give the baby up for adoption, but I couldn't go through with that decision either. I couldn't believe that anyone could love my baby as much as I do. It's hard to explain, but when you carry a life inside of you, you bond. I don't expect you to understand. Truly, I don't."

She gazes up into his eyes. "I tried to forget about you. I didn't want to burden you. It was beyond me to think that I could have both you and the baby. In the beginning, even Stan encouraged me to tell you. His words of wisdom were, 'Love conquers all.'" At the mention of Stan's name, she sees Brett's face harden. "Please don't hate him. He's a good man."

"He hid my letters. He was deceiving you. Why are you defending him?" Brett's voice is pleading. "Do you love him?"

"Stan has been so kind and generous. I am grateful for everything he has done for me, but gratitude isn't love. No, I don't love him."

"Do you still love me?" he asks. His eyes hold hers, and he squeezes her hands.

She touches his face. "Yes, I still love you. But how can you love me after all that I put you through?" A tear rolls down her face.

"I have to admit, you've put me through hell and back." He wipes her tear away with his finger. Then, he leans back on the bench and looks up into the sky. She watches him and thinks that his dimple is deeper. "I could tell that you were troubled. At first, I thought it was because you didn't want to take our relationship to the next level." He puts his arm around her. She reaches into her purse and takes out the small present.

"You can open the letters. Nothing has changed. And you do need to open your present." He motions toward the small box.

She takes the wrapping paper from the box and opens it. Inside is a small gold bracelet with trinity knots equally spaced around the chain.

"Wow, where did you find this? It matches my earrings and my necklace." She takes the bracelet out of the box and holds it up in the sunlight. "It's beautiful, thank you."

Brett pushes her hair back away from her ears, exposing her earrings. "I'm happy that you're still wearing them. Remember when you told me the meaning of the trinity knot? You said the circle on the knot represents the love that holds the family together. It's not the members of the family that hold the knot together, but it's the love that they have for each other. It's our love, Gabby. We can be a family: you, me, and the baby. I know I'm not the father, but I can't risk living without you."

She continues to hold up the gold bracelet. It glistens in the sun, but its sparkle seems dim compared to the glow she is feeling inside.

"Here, let's see if it fits." Brett takes the bracelet and latches it around her wrist.

"It's perfect," she says. "I love it." She leans over and gives him a light kiss.

"It doesn't surprise me that you couldn't go through with the abortion or the adoption. I know you, and I love you for who you are." He pats her hand. "You are the kindest, most caring, and giving person I have ever met. You, Miss Gabriella, will be a fabulous mother. That kid is pretty lucky. Have you told Richard?"

"I wasn't planning on telling him anything. Are you okay with that?"

"It's your call whether you want to involve Richard. Personally, I find him hard to stomach." He looks up into the trees before continuing. "I've done a lot of soul-searching in the past few months. I'm ready to settle down. I love working on the ranch instead of working at the country club. It's where my heart is. I know I love you, and I know that I can love your baby. We can do this. We can do this together."

She looks at him with admiration. "You really think so?"

"I don't think it. I know it." He looks at her and winks. "Promise me that the next baby will be our baby, yours and mine."

"That's an easy promise," she says. "It's easy because I love you."

"I love you more than I thought possible. I don't ever want to live without you again." He pulls her in, takes her face in his hands, and kisses her. Her body relaxes in his arms.

206

They get up and walk arm in arm through the park, enjoying each other's company even more than the picturesque landscape that surrounds them. Taking frequent breaks, they rest on benches, eat cotton candy, and catch up on the events in their lives since they parted. The rest stops remind Gabby of her pregnancy—a subject that both she and Brett have been avoiding. Even though she is enjoying their light conversation, they can't ignore discussing their future with a baby.

As he approaches, carrying a snow cone, she can tell from his walk and his demeanor that he has matured. She believes with all of her heart that he is ready to become a father, but she questions whether he can be a father to another man's child. However, his words tell her that he can.

"Here you go," he says. "A patriotic snow cone, only in D.C." He laughs as he hands her the iced red-white-and-blue treat.

"Brett, the baby is a boy."

He glances over at her, but remains silent.

"My due date is October 27. That's only three months away." His smile has disappeared. As she has feared, discussing the baby has caused their jovial mood to vanish.

"Okay," he finally answers and starts picking at his nails, avoiding eye contact.

"We need to talk about it," she continues, pressing him into a conversation.

"Okay."

"I know it's hard for you."

"I just need to get used to the idea. I came here unsure if you even wanted me in your life. I came here believing I was the father." He scoots over on the bench, away from her. "Gabby, in less than twenty-four hours, everything has changed."

She hears the disappointment in his voice.

"Learning the baby is Richard's and not mine was quite a shock, but I told you that I want you, even though the baby isn't mine."

"It's my child, too," she says, raising her voice, but then she backs down and says, "I'm really sorry. It's not your problem. It's mine. That's the reason I left Texas and the reason I left without telling you. You can walk away."

She sees the flash of anger on his face and wishes she could take back the words. He turns her face toward his.

"I hate when you seem to dismiss me. Walk away—how can you say that?" He shakes his head. "How many times do I need to tell you? Okay, I get it. You need reassurance that I can do this. I can, Gabby. I can because I don't want to live without you."

She reaches for him, pleading. "I'm so sorry this is happening to us." Tears fill her eyes.

"Gabby, if I love you, then your problem becomes our problem." He pulls her in close, and her head rests on his chest. "I told you I can do this."

She says, "Every day, I pray that this child will become a blessing, instead of a curse."

He kisses her cheek. "Me too. I pray the same."

Gabby wants to discuss more plans for their future; however, she is aware from his words that he still needs to finish grieving the loss of his child before he can accept her child.

Actually, he's handling the situation far better than she originally had expected. Now, she's the one who needs to be patient. Give him time to process everything. Meanwhile, she'll concentrate on the recovery of their relationship caused by the two-month separation. If their love for each other is as strong as he has professes, surely they can manage to get through this difficult time.

She looks down and swings her new bracelet around on her wrist, remembering the meaning of the trinity knot. It is the love that will keep them together. When she looks up, he's smiling at her.

"I'm glad you like it," he says. She gives him a hug.

Later that afternoon as they are having drinks at a local café, Brett takes her hand.

"I have some bad news."

"Oh." She searches his face for a clue.

"I leave for Texas this evening. Come back with me." His eyes seem to beg her. "I would stay longer if I could. I never want leave your side. But the boys, Rusty, and your dad, well…they're all counting on me."

She knits her brow. "I don't understand."

"The qualifying rounds for the rodeo are in a few days. I need to make the cut to participate in the regional event in two weeks. Come with me. I need you."

"I can't leave now. I would love to go back with you to Texas. We have so much to catch up on, but I can't just up and leave now."

"Why not?"

She looks down at her hands. "I have the exhibition, and Ella and Will are getting married in two weeks, and she has asked me to help coordinate the wedding and be her maid of honor." Brett's shoulders slump and he turns away. She feels his disappointment. "It's just two weeks. As soon as they say 'I do,' I'll be on the next plane back to Texas. I promise."

He hangs his head. "I know that she's your best friend."

"Thank you." She leans in to give him a kiss. "I'll miss you. I would rather be with you. You know that, right?"

"You'd better," he says, giving her a hug. "I understand, but I don't like it."

CHAPTER 24

Midland, Texas
Brett

Everyone from the small towns in west Texas attends the local rodeo. It's as much a tradition as attending church on Sunday mornings. As Brett walks the familiar grounds of his youth, the sweat trickles down his cheeks. Even though it is a scorching-hot summer day in early August, he knows the perspiration is connected to his nerves. His stomach has been aflutter since he woke up this morning.

Brett hasn't competed in an event in nearly two decades. He takes in a deep breath, hoping to find some relief; however, he finds none. He pauses before opening the door to the area underneath the stands where the cowboys congregate, and he scans the crowd. He wants to know where King and Rusty will be sitting. He rubs his chin when he finds them. God, he wishes Gabby were here. She would know just what to say to put his mind at ease.

Thinking about Gabby reminds him of their conversation earlier this morning over the phone.

Brett said, "Hey there. Good morning."

"Hey yourself. How are you?" Gabby asked.

"Nervous."

"I hear that you're ready for this, so relax. You're going to do great."

"The boys at the ranch informed me that there's a lot of money riding on the outcome. I wish they wouldn't do that. If they want to gamble, that's fine, just don't tell me about it," he said.

"It's all in fun," Gabby assured him. "Don't take it so seriously. Just do your best and have fun."

He remained quiet.

"They have seen how hard you've trained. It's their way of showing support. You should feel honored."

"I am honored, but I'm still nervous. I hope you're right."

"I know I'm right." She giggled. "I wish I could be there. You know that?"

"Yes, I understand all about Ella's wedding. I really do."

"I'm sorry her wedding is the same weekend as the rodeo."

"Even though Ella sent me an invitation, I'm sure that both Will and Stan would rather I not be there." He paused in deep thought. "It's probably for the best. The rodeo is the perfect excuse."

"I'll miss you."

"Thanks, I'll miss you too."

"Brett, have Jamie video your event so I can watch it later. Can you remember to ask her?"

"Rusty's already taking care of that, so he can show me exactly what I did wrong."

"Stop that. You need to be more positive. He's going to film because he is proud of you."

"You're right once again. Give my best to Ella and Will. I love you."

"I love you too."

"Oh, Gabby, one more thing, please. Stay clear of Stan."

"I can't avoid him. I'm the maid of honor, and he's the best man."

Brett rolled his eyes. "Don't remind me. But you know what I mean."

She said, "And I don't want to hear that you took up with some rodeo queen." She laughed, remembering their shared past.

"I already have my queen."

"Good luck!"

After finding King and Rusty, Brett hears the announcement for his event: "All cowboys for Event Fifteen, Calf Roping, please report to the registration desk."

It's show time. He clenches his hands.

After the event Brett feels a sense of belonging as he sees King, Rusty, and Jamie running toward him. He is relieved the calf-roping event is behind him. Jamie hugs him, and King and Rusty pat him on the shoulder. Brett sees their wide smiles, and he knows that he has earned their admiration.

"Well done. Well done," King shakes his hand. "You've made me so proud."

Rusty pipes up, "Three-tenths of a second is huge in this

business. It's your best time yet. I guess the adrenaline rush helps. Congratulations!" He winks at Brett.

Brett mumbles, "Thank you."

"Let's go and celebrate," King announces. "I haven't had a champion working for me in many years." He looks over at his foreman for an answer. "How long has it been?"

"Quite a while. I'll have to think about that." Rusty turns his attention back to Brett. "I knew you could do it. From the times I've been clocking for the past few weeks, it was a sure thing."

"Wish I could have been as sure as you."

"Let's go get that beer," says King. "I'm buying. It's gotta be quick because if I want to stay married, I need to catch a plane and get to a wedding."

King has chartered a private jet to get him to D.C. Even though his stepson's wedding is important, King wasn't about to miss his star ranch hand's performance at the rodeo. At first Rita had scowled at his idea of renting a plane, but he promised his bride that he would be there in plenty of time to witness his stepson's nuptials, and King was a man of his word.

CHAPTER 25

Washington, D.C.
Gabby

Y‌ou look beautiful," Gabby says as she adjusts the strap on Ella's wedding gown. "It's hard for me to believe that you're getting married." Ella looks at her reflection in the mirror, and Gabby sees her smile. "And you look so happy."

"If you can't believe it, I can't believe it. I'm a little scared, to be honest. Everything has happened so fast. I never thought that I would beat you to the altar."

"You and Will are so cute together." Her best friend is radiant in her white gown with soft blush-pink ribbons threaded through the lace. She and Ella have talked about this day since... well, since forever. Gabby remembers an evening when they were sorority sisters.

"Look at this one, Gabby." Ella pointed to a page in the bridal magazine and giggled. "It looks more like a dress a gal would wear to a funeral, not her wedding." She took a sip of her wine as Gabby peered over her shoulder at the page.

215

"Oh, yuck," Gabby squealed. "I see what you mean. Do some brides really wear black?"

"According to this article, it's the newest trend. It may be a trend but on my big day, I'm going to wear a traditional white gown." Ella flipped through more pages and gasped. "Oh, Gabby, check this one out. It's perfect!" She pointed to a white chiffon gown that had rows of layered lace around the hem.

"You would look amazing in that dress," Gabby said.

She remembers at the time thinking it to be the most beautiful gown. Now, as she gazes upon her best friend, just minutes before the bride will take that long-anticipated short walk down the aisle, Gabby thinks this dress is similar to that very dress Ella deemed perfect nearly a decade before.

"Gabby, can you straighten my tiara?" Ella is standing facing the full-length mirror. "Yes, Will is perfect. He is my Mr. Right." She continues to stare into the glass. "Why am I so anxious?"

After adjusting Ella's tiara, Gabby keeps her hands on Ella's shoulders. "You may have beaten me to the altar but not to motherhood," she says. "This little guy is sure moving around today." She places her hand on her stomach and smiles. She is in the same dark purple dress that she wore at her art reception. However, her stomach has grown considerably in the past two weeks. She's thankful that the dress still fits.

"Stan tells me that Will is equally as jittery," Gabby says. "The minister is here, and your mother and my parents are seated." She giggles. "It's funny that after you're married, we'll be family. You will be my step-sister-in-law." She giggles again. "Here are your flowers."

She hands Ella a bouquet of white roses and white daisies with hints of baby's breath tied with a lavender ribbon.

Ella asks, "You have Will's ring?"

"It's right here," Gabby waves the plain gold band in front of Ella and gives her one last hug. "Okay, best friend, are you ready?"

"I'm so glad that you're here. I'm so lucky to have you. Thanks, Gabby."

Gabby embraces her again. "I wouldn't miss it!"

"Okay, let's go!" Ella says.

They exit the room arm in arm.

Gabby has stayed in Washington for the past two weeks to help Ella plan her wedding. When Ella first said that she and Will didn't want to wait, Gabby never thought that their wedding would take place this soon. It is a small affair with less than fifty guests attending. In addition to family, most of the guests are friends of Will, with just a handful of Ella's family and coworkers.

The temperature is perfect for the evening wedding on the hotel's back patio. Slowly and with pride, Gabby makes her way down the aisle as the harpist plays. Her nosegay of daisies shakes as she sees Stan standing next to Will at the front of the archway adorned with flowers. Both men are dashing in their black tuxedos. Stan smiles and nods. She returns his smile and approaches the first row of chairs; Ella's mother is seated on the left, and Rita and her daddy are on the right. King steps into the aisle and brushes Gabby's cheek with a kiss before she continues walking to the front of the balcony. Her daddy cleans up well; only his callused hands alert others that he has a life outside the suit he sports.

The music pauses but then picks up the tempo and volume as Ella enters the room. Gabby thinks her best friend glows and deserves to be happy.

As all eyes are on Ella and her father as they approach, Gabby steals a glance at Stan, and he stares back. Seeing his serious face, as if he is saddled with great sadness, she turns away. Her heart aches for him as she is laced with guilt from the pain her indecision caused. Stan has been collateral damage in her crisis.

During the reception, right after the wedding, Gabby stands on the balcony of the hotel. She needs to distance herself from the noise and craziness. Minutes ago, Will and Ella cut and shared their cake. Now, Ella is getting ready to throw her bouquet, and Gabby doesn't want to be included in the rush of young, giggling girls. She looks out into the lights of the city and enjoys the light summer breeze.

Thinking of the happy couple makes her feel lonely. She looks up to the sky, touches her trinity knot necklace, and makes a wish on a star. After she wishes for Will and Ella to have a great life, she then wishes the same for her and Brett's happiness. She misses Brett. He could have returned to Washington after the rodeo on the plane with her daddy, but they made a mutual decision that his presence would create tension and it was best for him to stay in Texas. Even though Ella invited him, from the events over the past few weeks leading up to the wedding, Gabby was well aware that Will and Stan did not share that same opinion. She shivers, recalling Stan's serious look earlier as Ella and Will said their vows.

She's anxious to be leaving tomorrow to return to Texas. Deep in thought, she jumps when there is a light tap on her shoulder. He stands so close that she is uncomfortable.

"What are you doing out here? The couple is getting ready to leave," Stan says.

Gabby turns to face him. "I was wishing on a star."

"Oh, yes. I should have known. I'm aware of your love of stars from the ones you made me put on the ceiling in your room. Does it work?"

"Does what work?"

"Wishing on a star."

"It doesn't hurt to try." She gazes up into the heavens again.

He frowns. "You're right, it can't hurt to try. However, somehow, I don't think my wish will come true." He looks out over the city. "You look beautiful...as always," he says. "How are you feeling?"

"The baby is great, just a couple of months to go." Her teeth chatter because the night temperature is dropping. He takes off his suit coat and wraps it around her shoulders. He pauses just a bit too long, which makes her uneasy.

"The wedding was wonderful. The whole time I stood there listening to Will and Ella as they confessed their love for one another, I was thinking of you."

Unable to face him, she turns and continues to gaze out into the night sky.

"I wish it could have been us today. I still love you," he says.

"Don't," she responds, not daring to look in his direction.

"Anyway, I had to say it. When I look up to the stars and make a wish, I wish for you to be mine. I can't help it. It's the way I feel."

"Stan, you are a kind, gentle soul. You'll find your true love someday."

"You promise?" He leans against the railing, facing her. "I hope you're right. Getting over you won't be any time soon, I'm afraid. We'd better get inside."

He offers her his arm and escorts her back to the reception.

"Bye, Ella. Enjoy your honeymoon." Gabby hugs and kisses her best friend one more time. "Take good care of her, Will," she adds as she gives Will one last embrace. Rita and King are also waiting in line to extend their wishes. Gabby notices that Stan has moved over to the side.

Ella and Will wave as the limousine slowly accelerates and turns the corner out of view.

"They make such a lovely couple," Rita says.

"They sure do," Gabby agrees. "I'll miss her."

"That makes sense since the two of you have been friends for quite a while. But life goes on, and time has a way of changing things." Rita puts her arm around Gabby's waist. "You will be so busy with your new little guy you won't have much time to miss anyone. Your whole world will be changing."

"You think so?"

"I know because one of my little guys just got in that car. There were days when I thought he would never grow up. But time goes on." Rita's voice cracks, and when Gabby looks over, she sees a tear splash down Rita's cheek.

"Ah, Rita, don't cry." Gabby wraps her arms around her.

"They are happy tears. I'm really happy that they found each other." Rita sniffles and says, "I get so emotional these days."

"Me too!" Gabby holds her stomach and wipes away a small tear.

The next day at the airport, Rita and Gabby are sitting at the gate waiting for their flight back to Texas. Gabby sees her daddy pacing the long corridor. He hates to fly, so the pacing helps him to get rid of his anxiety. This brings to mind just how important the rodeo was to her daddy since he was willing to take a private jet to D.C. to witness Ella and Will tie the knot.

Rita puts her magazine in her lap and says, "The wedding was beautiful: my Will, so handsome, and Ella—well, as pretty as a princess. When my boy makes up his mind, he doesn't fool around." She looks over the rims of her glasses, expecting Gabby to respond.

"Ella is equally as impulsive," Gabby says. "When she told me they were getting married in two weeks, it surprised me as well." She turns in her chair to face Rita. "I'm glad we were able to get everything arranged with such little notice. All the details seemed to fall into place like it was meant to be."

"I know that Will is very thankful that you stayed to help Ella."

"Ella's my best friend. I wouldn't have it any other way."

Rita takes her hand. "You're a good girl. I know it was hard for you to stay here and send Brett back alone. The two of you have a lot of catching up to do."

"You're right about that, but I think Brett needed some time alone to process everything. He says the right words but I want him to take time to feel the meaning of those words in his heart."

"Oh..." Rita says, lifting an eyebrow.

"He came here thinking I was carrying his child. From what he says, I think he was actually excited about the idea of being a father."

"Well, none of that has changed." Rita shakes her head. "He's still going to be a father."

"You're right, that hasn't changed, but he knows that he isn't the baby's real father. It's like he's grieving a loss and I pray that with time he will learn to love my baby...our baby, as if it was his."

"Mr. Dimples will come around. I'm sure of it." Then she says, "Brett will be easier to fix than Stan. I'm worried about him."

"I never meant to hurt him, Rita. He was good to me. He is a kind soul."

"That he is. That's the reason I'm concerned," Rita says thoughtfully. She looks away. Gabby feels that Rita holds her responsible for causing Stan's pain. Hearing the truth hurts.

"Getting over you will be tough," Rita turns to face her. "I warned Stan, weeks ago when I first learned that he was falling for you." Rita's stare burns, and the fire seems to go straight to Gabby's soul. "But Stan knew best. He was out to prove me wrong."

Unable to stand the heat, Gabby looks down to her lap. "He'll find someone, someone who deserves him." She twirls the trinity knot bracelet around on her wrist.

"Is that new?" Rita asks.

"Yes. Brett gave it to me. He gave the trinity knot a new message. It now stands for our family."

Rita knits her brow.

"Our new family—Brett, me, and my baby."

"Really?" Rita raises her eyebrows.

"Rita, it's a good thing. I have a confession. When Daddy married you, part of me was happy; however, another part of me was very sad. I felt he was forgetting—forgetting my mother and forgetting our family." She takes Rita's hand and squeezes.

"Now, I realize that life offers many opportunities for love. Just like Daddy has added you to our lives, I'll be adding Brett and my little one. Life is full of trinity knots. It would be a shame to limit ourselves to just one. This bracelet has several trinity knots, and it reminds me to be open to love."

She rotates the bracelet around her wrist again. "Rita, thank you for coming into our lives. You make Daddy very happy. You have been there for Brett and for me. You will be an awesome grandmother." She squeezes Rita's hand again and smiles.

King returns with three cups of coffee. Gabby is grateful for his timing. She doesn't know what more she can say; however, she feels Rita accepted her apology. Time has a way of healing and Gabby prays that with time Stan will heal and find happiness with someone to love as well.

PART IV

CHAPTER 26

Texas
Gabby

It's a lazy summer Sunday afternoon at the ranch, and the first chance that Gabby and Brett have been able to spend time together since she returned. They've taken the Jeep loaded with a blanket and picnic basket to go to Gabby's favorite spot down by the lake.

She spreads the blanket under the tall oak, and the cardinals perched on the limbs above welcome her home with their song.

"I've really missed Texas," she says. "I'll take the heat over the humidity of the East Coast any day." She reaches into the basket and hands Brett a brisket sandwich.

"I'm glad you're back, too." Brett stuffs a pickle into his mouth.

She knows he is happy because his dimple is more prominent when the corners of his mouth curve slightly upward.

"I'm sorry you missed Ella's wedding. It was wonderful...so romantic. She was the radiant bride, and Will was so dashing. They make a great couple."

"I'm sure I wasn't missed. How was Stan?" Brett asks. The slight upward curve that she noticed earlier is gone.

"Stan?" Gabby says, surprised.

"You're talking about the wedding and how romantic it was, so how was Stan? Did you dance with him? Did he kiss you?"

"Oh, I get it. You're jealous." She smacks him on his arm and smiles.

"Don't I have a right to be?" He takes a large gulp of his beer. "He loves you, Gabby."

"He was sad. I assured him that his true love is out there waiting for him. I never meant to hurt him. I feel bad about that." She frowns.

"Hey, I shouldn't have said anything. It's a beautiful sunny day and we're here together—let's talk about something else." His smile is back.

They finish their lunch with only small talk. She snuggles her head on his chest and closes her eyes. She remembers how she longed for this moment those long months when they were apart.

Breaking the silence, she says, "Help me up." She sits up and puts her hand out so Brett can hoist her to her feet. Immediately, she strips down to her bathing suit. She feels his intense stare.

"I've been worried about your reaction, you know, seeing me like this." She rubs her stomach. "I know I'm not a pretty sight."

"I didn't mean to stare. It's just that, well, I've never seen a pregnant woman before. Well, not one in a bikini."

She sees that he is looking over to the lake in an attempt to avoid looking into her eyes. "It's the only suit I can get into." It hurts to see him react this way, but it is the reaction that she has been dreading. It's best to confront this now. If they're going to have a future together raising a baby, this is just the first small hurdle in their journey. "I'm going for a swim," she announces. "Are you coming?"

Brett's face sports a surprised look but she doesn't wait for his response. She skips down the bank of the lake and hops onto the small wooden dock. She hears him call after her.

"Hey, Gabby, wait for me." She turns to see him pulling his shirt over his head as he runs toward her.

"Do you think it's safe for you to swim?" he yells as if he needs to protect her.

She acts like she doesn't hear him and dangles her feet into the water. She glances in his direction one last time before she jumps into the water.

"This feels great," she says after resurfacing. "Are you coming?" she teases. "Get in here."

He flashes a big grin and does a cannonball that sprays water all over her. She laughs as she feels him surface next to her.

"Feels nice, doesn't it?"

"Yes, it does but not as good as it feels holding you."

It makes her happy to hear his words, and she leans her head into his chest as he wraps his arms around her waist. His warm breath on her hair feels nice, and they float together. She knows Brett needs to get used to her pregnant body; however, this small gesture gives her hope that he is willing to try. And for that, she is ever so grateful.

On an impulse, she breaks free and splashes him, kicking her way back to the dock. Swimming to the ladder, she lifts herself out of the water and lies on her back. The warmth of the wood gives her comfort. She takes in a deep breath, and for the first time her body and soul feel what her mind has known, she is home.

As the sound of him swimming gets nearer, she feels him splash water on her stomach.

Still in the water, he looks up at her on the dock. "What's it like to be pregnant?" He squints in the bright sun.

She turns and props up on her elbow, peering down at him, grinning.

"Now, it's wonderful, but I'm told that won't last. It will get harder as time goes on until I deliver. However, at first it wasn't much fun at all."

"What do you mean?"

"I was so sick, nauseated and retching. It was pretty miserable, and I was tired. It was a tiredness I've never experienced. Combine all of that with the confusion and disappointment ..."

Brett cocks his head to the side as if he doesn't understand, so she continues, "I wasn't happy learning that the baby wasn't yours. It was pretty traumatic." She swallows hard and bites her lip before turning her head so he doesn't see.

He climbs out of the water.

"Hey, I'm sorry I wasn't there for you, but I'm here now." She feels his touch and reaches for his hand.

"Thank you." She inhales deeply. "I want us to work. It won't be easy, but if we have each other, we can do this."

He hoists her up, and they embrace. After returning to their blanket, his head lowers, and his lips find hers, giving her reassurance that they will be all right.

"Make love to me," she whispers, then kisses him on the neck.

"I can't do that," he says, looking away. "You're pregnant."

"So," she giggles, pulling him closer. "I still can have sex." She reaches down and strokes him. His breathing quickens, and she feels him getting hard. "Make love to me."

"But I don't want to hurt the baby."

She turns his face to her. "Brett, look at me. You're not going to hurt the baby. I promise." She eagerly kisses him again, offering encouragement. "I've missed you. Make love to me." She snuggles into his body and continues to stroke him. She'll make him an offer he would be out of his mind to refuse.

CHAPTER 27

Gabby

The hotel lobby at the Driscoll in Austin is bustling with action. People are scurrying in and out, and the bellmen are hustling with heaps of luggage. Gabby sits patiently, watching as she waits. Usually, Brett is the one who does the waiting, but today it is her turn.

Yes, today was the second success for Brett on the rodeo circuit. Now, to celebrate they are going out on the town with King, Rita, Rusty, and Jamie. Gabby hasn't seen her daddy this involved in the rodeo in many years. She feels certain that it is the thought of having a champion working at his ranch. Combining King's enthusiasm with the added expectations of Rusty, she is sure that Brett is feeling the pressure to do his best by continuing his winning streak.

Sometimes when these men get into a conversation about the rodeo and its events, she listens and rolls her eyes as it seems that they tend to embellish what actually takes place. But it's all in fun. She is thankful that her daddy and Brett get along so well with common interests. The corners of her mouth turn upward, and she pats her stomach because she knows that in a few years, there will be another little man joining them in the comradery. Her boy will bring the family so much joy.

The loud voices from the crowd gathered at the hotel's entrance cause Gabby to turn in her chair. The city is known for its film-making and also for its music scene, so celebrities are frequently spotted in local venues. However, walking through the hotel doors is a man who steals her breath away. Oh, my God, she thinks and slaps her hand over her mouth. It's not an actor or a famous musician.

It is Richard.

She shakes her head and looks down. She was bound to run into him sooner or later.

At first, it appears he is preoccupied with a reporter and the news crew. He must be doing an interview about his campaign for the evening news. She takes a deep breath, thinking she will be spared a confrontation, but a few seconds later, Richard turns and locks his eyes on her. He starts walking in her direction.

"Gabriella, imagine finding you here," he says boisterously. She feels his eyes scanning her from her face to her feet and then back again. "Your dad must have passed on the information that I was campaigning here." He leans forward with a smile on his face and then he whispers in her ear, "So it really is true."

She feels his hot breath on her face, and it makes her skin crawl. She stands still; however, her mind is telling her to get out of there and fast. She stares at him. He seems unable to mask his emotions as he bursts out in laughter.

"We could have been campaigning together. We made a really

good team—great, in fact. Well, that was before you started whoring around." He clicks his tongue against the roof of his mouth, making a high-pitched sound.

He touches her face and lifts her chin up. "It's disappointing. You had so much potential."

"You bastard," she yells with detestation, not caring who overhears their conversation.

"Careful, careful, Gabby. I don't believe that someone in your present condition ought to be using such language."

She reaches out to strike him, but he grabs her forearm.

"Should I be calling over the camera crew to get your little tantrum documented?" He continues to hold on to her arm.

"I think you should take your hand away ... now," Brett demands as he steps between them.

"And if I don't?" Richard sneers "What are you going to do about it? Start some brawl like a stupid cowboy?" Richard releases her arm and shuffles back a few inches. "Go ahead. I could use the free advertising, and it may even get me some votes."

Gabby is grateful that Brett came to her defense; however, now she needs to separate the two men before a fight breaks out and is plastered all over the evening news.

"Brett," she says, taking his arm. "Let's go."

Brett continues to hold his stance and his stare.

"Brett, please, let's go," She pulls on his arm again.

Brett takes her hand and pushes past Richard. "You're such an ass."

Richard yells to them as they head for the door. "Remember to cast your vote for Richard, Richard Wright, the right choice."

Outside the main doors of the hotel, Brett pulls Gabby to the side.

"What was that all about?"

"Nothing," she lies.

"Nothing," he repeats. "It sure looked like something to me." He pushes a loose strand of hair behind her ear. "Gabby, tell me. For you to try to slap him, it was definitely something."

She tries to fight back tears, but her lip starts to quiver and her body shakes. He holds her.

She sniffles. "I shouldn't let him get to me like this."

He continues to hold her and stroke her back.

"I'm so sorry. He's such a jerk. Tell me what he said."

In between sobs she says, "He called me a whore and then referred to the baby as a bastard." Brett holds her more tightly. "Thanks for not hitting him." She sniffles again.

"I should have," He looks back into the hotel as if second-guessing his decision to walk away.

"I don't want any attention drawn to us: you, me, and especially the baby. The more distance we put between Richard and us. the better off everyone will be."

He looks down at his watch, "We're late. Your dad will start to worry." He wipes her tears away with his finger. He wraps his arm around her waist. "Forget about him. Come along, pretty lady, we've got some celebrating to do." There is a bounce in his step.

CHAPTER 28

Gabby

It is a slow day at Art Smart. The over one-hundred-degree temperatures of the Texas summer must be keeping folks off the streets and in their air-conditioned homes. Gabby has been managing the gallery for the past few days because Rita and her daddy have slipped away to the coast for a long weekend at the beach. Married life seems to agree with them.

Thinking of marriage, Gabby is reminded of Ella. She should give her a call. Even though Ella is at work, Gabby punches her number into her phone.

"Hey, Ella, it's Gabby. How are you?"

"Gabby! It's good to hear your voice. I'm fine. Miss you, though."

"How's Will?"

"He's really wonderful. I'm a lucky girl."

"Sounds like you're still on your honeymoon."

"I wish that were true, but we both had to get back to work. We'll be married three weeks tomorrow. I bought Will the cutest card."

Gabby smiles as she twirls her hair around her finger. Ella is such a romantic.

"It seems longer," Gabby says.

"Hey, how's the little guy?"

"Getting bigger every day." Gabby looks down at her protruding stomach. "Oh, my belly button is now an outie."

"Yuck. Did you pick a name yet?"

"I have a few in mind, but I haven't decided on anything yet."

"Gabby, I saw Richard on the news."

"Really? In D.C.?" Gabby is surprised.

"Yes, the local station was reviewing all the candidates nationwide and they had a special segment on the election in Texas. They said he has a good chance of winning."

"My daddy says the same thing. Brett and I ran into him downtown last weekend."

"How did that go? Brett and Richard still hate each other?"

Gabby chooses her words carefully. "Same old Richard. Some people never change. He seems to enjoy being in the spotlight." She hesitates, then asks, "How's Stan?"

There is a brief pause before Ella answers. "He seems kind of depressed. He's really quiet. Will and I invited him to dinner a few days ago, and he just sat there. It's sad."

Gabby looks down and pinches her lip. "I'm sorry to hear that."

"It will just take time, Gabby. Hey, my other line is ringing. Got to go. Bye."

She hears the click. The news about Stan causes her concern. However, she is the last person that Stan would want lending an ear or giving him advice. She recalls Ella's words, "It will just take time."

Putting her phone in her pocket, she rubs her arms and takes in a deep breath waiting for the clock to chime on the hour. Business seems even slower after two o'clock in the afternoon, so that is when she will slip into the back room and paint.

Today she can hardly wait to get the brush in her hand. The first painting in her new series is coming along nicely, and she feels certain that she will make her self-imposed deadline. Even though she put the first strokes of paint to the canvas a few days ago, the design has been playing in her head for the past month. It was Ella's wedding that initially inspired the idea, and since then she has become obsessed with it.

Now, it feels good for her to get the opportunity to see that idea spring to life. Unlike the Trinity Knot series that she painted to heal her from her grief or her Zeppelin Bend series that depicted the union of two families, this new series, The Hitch series, will represent her future. It may become the most important painting series she has ever created.

For the premiere painting in the series, she chose colors that provoke feelings of joy and happiness. When first applying the many shades of gold to the canvas, creating a background that many would interpret as nature's landscape, the color caused her heart to leap with delight. Encouraged by this feeling, she kept adding more and more layers of yellow paint, making the background a complex myriad of different tones of golden yellows that would enhance the simpler but all-important main subject.

Now, Gabby is ready to paint the knot, the symbol of commitment to a permanent relationship with Brett. Of all the hues she can create by mixing paint, what color would evoke a feeling of eternity? When she closes her eyes, it's the color of his eyes that she envisions—those deep emerald irises. She smiles as she remembers the image of an excited Brett just this spring, who lifted her off her feet and twirled her in the air. He had a sparkle in his eyes when he asked her to commit to their relationship. At that time his question had taken her by surprise, and she could not give him the answer that he desperately wished to hear.

Nonetheless, as the season changed from spring to summer, she is aware that her relationship with Brett has also changed. Will Brett still be excited to share his future with her and her child?

She closes her eyes and recalls all of the times that she visualized a romantic engagement scene—the scene where the man gets down on one knee and speaks words of love, and places a forever diamond on her finger. Never, in all of her dreams, did she ever envision a pregnant woman popping the question, but here she is, and that is precisely what she intends to do. She will give a voice to these deep feelings of love that she has for this man—the man who owns those intense emerald eyes.

First, she must finish this painting as it will be her gift, promising him her love for eternity. This painting needs to be perfect.

CHAPTER 29

Gabby

Once again Gabby calls Brett's cell to remind him of their date. She knows he's busy at the ranch, and the cell phone signal is poor, but she leaves a text. She's in a hurry as she completes a few errands in town before driving out to the ranch. She hopes her new green dress doesn't wrinkle during the two-hour car ride to the ranch.

In her car she rechecks her list. She has his favorite beer and chocolate-chip cookies in the passenger's seat of the car. Jamie is preparing the rest of the dinner, and Rusty has orders to get the site ready.

At last, she arrives at the ranch and hurries into the tan stucco ranch house carrying her parcels.

"Gabby, is that you?" Jamie yells, entering the living room from the kitchen. "Look at you, child ... so pretty and so big." She touches Gabby's belly. "You've doubled in size since I last saw you. My, oh my, your dear sweet mama must be looking down from heaven smiling."

The mention of Anna causes Gabby to reach for her trinity knot necklace.

"I do miss her," she says, looking around the room. The entire main floor is decorated with the new furniture that Rita had chosen. She sucks in her breath.

"I know it looks different." It's as if Jamie is reading Gabby's mind. "But I'm getting used to it. Sometimes change is good, Miss Gabby." Gabby chooses to ignore the remark and get back to more pressing matters.

"Is everything ready?" She glances down at her phone. "I'm running out of time. Brett will be finished with work before I know it. It took longer to get everything done than I planned."

Jamie takes Gabby's hands in her own. "No need to worry. It's perfect. I just came back an hour ago. Even the weather is on your side, a beautiful evening tonight. No chance of rain tomorrow."

"Thank you, Jamie. I know how much effort you put into this evening."

"You're quite welcome, but your dad is really the one to thank. He's been dealing with the officials to get the proper permits. Not to mention, keeping Mr. Dimples busy and away from the site." Jamie puts her hands on her hips. "I made Rusty swear to me that he wouldn't breathe a word. That man is worse than a woman when it comes to keeping his mouth shut." She giggles.

Gabby looks down.

"Hey, why the long face? You don't seem too excited."

"I'm worried about Brett. What if he says no?"

"Hush, child, there's no need to worry. Look at you!" She gives Gabby a motherly hug. "Everything will be fine. Mark my words."

It's a little past five o'clock when Gabby sees the familiar gait of the man she loves round the path from the ranch house toward the Jeep. From his clothing, she knows that he has showered and changed. She stares at him in disbelief that he will be all hers. She lifts her shoulders back and takes a deep breath.

"Hi," she calls and then waves.

"Hey there," he says as he gets nearer. "Don't you look nice." He pulls her in close for a kiss. "You smell good, too." He looks at her at arm's length. "Hey, I thought we were having dinner here."

"We are. I wanted you to see my new dress." She twirls around. "Do you like it? It matches the color of your eyes."

"It's nice. Anything you wear looks great."

"We're having a picnic." She claps her hands together.

"I should have guessed. I didn't bring my bathing suit."

"You can skinny-dip. I wouldn't mind," she teases with a sparkle in her eyes. "You ready? Jamie helped. Picnic basket, blanket, and a cooler with your favorite beer."

Gabby throws the keys at him. "I hope you're hungry because Jamie has packed enough for an entire army."

"Starved, as always after a long day's work." Brett sits behind the wheel of the Jeep and she climbs into the passenger seat.

"Buckle up," he says.

"Remember I'm pregnant, so easy on the accelerator, cowboy, or this baby may come out early." She winks at him.

"Where're we going?"

She flashes him a grin. "You know, silly." She taps his arm. "To my favorite place."

"Yes, ma'am." He reaches over to hold her hand.

When they round the bend with the lake in front of them, Brett sees the wooden stakes with pink ribbons at the top.

"What's all this?" he asks as he parks the Jeep and turns off the ignition.

"Grab a beer, and I'll explain." She motions toward the cooler. She's so excited to be able to give the details about the plans for the house that they will build together, if he consents to her proposal. "Come, walk with me."

She walks to the stake closest to the Jeep. Brett follows.

"This stake marks the corner of the house. It will face east, so when you sit on the porch in the morning to have coffee, it will be warm and sunny, but then, in the evening after dinner, the porch will be in the shade, and the chairs will face the lake." She grabs his hand.

Brett takes a swig of beer and follows her. Still holding his hand, she walks to another stake.

"This one marks the back of the house. Even though the house faces the lake, I still want a pool and a hot tub. Those will be behind the back deck around here." She points with her arm gesturing to the right. "And all that flat land there where the pasture and prickly pear are—there is enough room for a tennis court."

He smiles. "A tennis court out here on the ranch." He scratches his head and raises an eyebrow.

"You and I both enjoy playing," she explains. "Daddy didn't seem to have a problem with it."

"Your dad?" Brett looks at her with his head cocked to one side. "Why do I get the feeling that everyone seems to know about this but me?"

"Well, what do you think?" She bites her lip, waiting for his reply.

"Of what ... the tennis court? If that's what you want—"

"No, not just the tennis court but the whole plan ... the house here by the lake?"

"Why ask me? Sounds like you and your dad have it all planned."

She hears the hurt in his voice. This isn't going at all like she had hoped. She wanted him to be excited about their future house.

She reaches for his hand and then takes a deep breath in an effort to compose herself. She gazes up into his eyes. Her heart is pounding and her voice quivers. With a soft voice she asks, "Brett, will you marry me?"

There, she has said it. Closing her eyes, she looks away.

He stares at her with wide eyes and leans back. "What?" he asks as if in disbelief. "I could barely hear you, but did you just ask me to marry you?" He shakes his head.

"Yes, I believe that I did." She giggles.

"Wow, this is a surprise." He looks into her brown eyes. "I need to think about this," he says with a big grin that accentuates his dimple.

Gabby hangs her head. Unsure of how much time has passed, she compares it to a lifetime. Her heart is still beating fast, and she can feel the beads of perspiration on her skin. Now, what is she to do?

"Okay," he says in a very matter-of-fact tone.

"Okay, what?" she asks, daring to look into his emerald eyes again.

"Okay, I'll marry you." His eyes sparkle, and he wears a big grin.

"You will?"

"Isn't that the answer you want to hear? I'm so confused." He shakes his head.

"Yes, you said yes." Her hands go to her mouth. "You said yes."

"Come here." He takes her in his arms. He lifts her off her feet. Her breathing quickens as she looks into his eyes. He puts her back down on the ground.

"Ask me again," he says, beaming at her.

This time, the words are easier to say.

"Brett, I love you. I want to be with you forever. Will you marry me?" This time the words flow out of her mouth with more confidence.

"Yes, I'll marry you. I love you, Gabby." He holds her face between his hands.

"I love you so much." She lets out a deep breath, and she can feel the goose bumps on her arms. Right now, she's so happy. He has given her her dream. He holds her tightly, and she smells his spicy scent. She hangs onto him for dear life, and her emotions run out of control. Unable to hold back her tears, she starts to sob.

"Hey, hey, what's this?" He holds her at arm's length and studies her face.

"I'm so sorry," she sobs. If she had confided in him months ago, would he have had the same reaction? Now that her deepest wish is coming true, she can sigh in relief, but the guilt she feels over the pain she caused him overtakes her. She can't control her blubbering.

"I thought you would be happy. Why are you sorry?" He looks so confused.

"I'm so sorry I hurt you. I'm sorry I didn't confide in you months ago. I'm sorry I didn't believe in us." She shifts her weight from one foot to the other. "Night after night, when I wished on a star, I wished for this moment. I wished for us, you and me, and I wished for our family: you, me, and the baby. I underestimated our love. I didn't know what to do."

"Hey, none of that matters now. If anything, everything that we've gone through has made us stronger." He wipes her tears away with his hand. "It made me face reality. I'm so happy working here at the ranch with Rusty and your dad. I'm happy to be competing on the rodeo circuit. I would have never made this change on my own. And I have to admit, I was upset that Richard is the father. I still am a bit, but there's nothing anyone can do about that." He looks away into the horizon and pauses before continuing.

"However, when I saw you and Stan getting out of the taxi at the gallery, and I saw how happy he was to be with you, I was so jealous. It was as if someone knocked some sense into me. I thought if Stan could love you and the baby, then I needed to man up. I wasn't going to let him steal you away. I knew that he had feelings for you from his reaction when your name was mentioned the night of your dad's wedding. It became so obvious that night that there was a chance that I could lose you."

"I don't ever want us to be apart again," Gabby says and gives him another hug, placing her cheek on his chest.

"That's good by me."

Gabby walks over to the Jeep and gets the canvas she had hidden earlier behind the seat. "This is for you." She proudly hands him the painting covered in brown paper and tied with twine.

"What's this?"

"Open it."

Brett unwraps the canvas. "What's this?" he asks again, holding the canvas out. "I can tell it's another knot, but I know you well enough to know that it means something special."

"You're so smart." She takes the canvas from him and places it against the old oak tree facing them. "This is the first of my new Hitch series. It represents our commitment to each other."

"That's very clever. A hitch, you say." He rubs his chin.

"So, you like it?" she asks.

"I love it! I'm going to love being hitched to you!"

She leans over and kisses him on the cheek.

"That is not going to do." His dimple is deep and he pulls her in tight. She holds onto his bicep. Feeling the muscle, she is reminded that he is strong and will keep her safe. His kiss is full of hunger and begs for more of her. She holds him a little tighter and is certain that he is her Mr. Right.

Minutes later he takes out the blanket and the picnic basket from the Jeep. They spread the blanket over the ground. Before sitting, Gabby gets the tube with the architectural plans out of the Jeep and finds rocks to hold down the corners to keep it flat.

"What's that?" He motions toward the plastic tube.

"Those are the plans for our house. We can go over them later. This is a rough draft and we can add specific details to make it our perfect home. We can add or change anything that you'd like. I want our house to be perfect, perfect for both of us."

They pore over the plans while enjoying the delicious meal that Jamie prepared for the couple on this memorable evening.

"I think I ate too much." Brett lies back on the blanket and rubs his stomach. "It sure was good."

"Yes, it was. I don't think I can eat another bite either." She starts putting their plates and forks back into the basket. "Ouch," she cries, holding her stomach.

Brett looks over at her with concern.

"It's just the baby. He gave me quite a kick."

"Can I feel?" he asks. She has never suggested that he feel the baby move. She remembers how excited Stan was after he felt the baby kick. How could she have overlooked allowing Brett the same experience?

She reaches over for his hand and places it on her stomach.

"We just have to wait. I never know when he's going to do it." She scooches closer to him and props her head on his chest. They lie facing the western sky, and the sun is just starting to set over the horizon.

"Brett, have you thought of any names for our baby?"

"Names … no. I thought you would take care of that."

She reaches over and messes up his hair. "You have to help. Surely, you can think of a few boys' names that you like. What was your father's name?"

He smiles. "My father's name was Jacob."

"That's a solid name."

"It's an old name. I don't think anyone names their son Jacob these days."

"That's what makes it so special. You don't want a name that's popular because when he gets to school, half a dozen other boys in the class will have the same name. We want something different."

"What about naming him after your dad? Wayne. Your dad would really like that."

"I don't think my dad ever really loved his name. People always refer to him by his last name, however, we could use Wayne as a middle name. Jacob Wayne. I kind of like the way it sounds." She repeats it again, "Jacob Wayne."

"So will his full name be Jacob Wayne King or Jacob Wayne Matthews?"

"That will depend."

"Depend on what?" He rubs his chin as if in thought.

"That will depend on when we get married. If we get married before or after the baby is born. Now, we need to set a date."

"But you just asked me tonight. Oh, my—" Brett's mouth opens, his eyes wide.

"You felt him?" Gabby sits up.

"Yes. Doesn't that feel weird?"

"At first, when he was smaller, it felt like a tiny butterfly flutter, and now that he is bigger, I enjoy feeling him move. It reassures me that he's healthy and doing fine."

As the darkness approaches, Gabby looks up into the trees. The solar-powered fairy lights are shining. She had Rusty hang them, and their tiny twinkles cause her to grin.

"It's magical … and so romantic." She cuddles up closer to Brett and motions for him to glance up.

"Tonight is perfect." She strokes his face. "Thank you for loving me enough to have me for your wife and for agreeing to be a father to Jacob."

"I should be the one thanking you. None of this would be possible without your forgiveness. Thank you for giving me a second chance. I love you, Gabby King."

Holding each other close, they look up into the night sky.

"Let's make a wish. You make one and I'll make one." She squeezes her eyes tight. "Now, it's your turn."

"I already got my wish." He chuckles. "I got you and that's all I need. Those wishes on stars really do come true. Life is pretty darn good."

"Yes, life is pretty darn good. Now that it's dark, how about some lovin', cowboy?"

About the Author

Donna Overly is a graduate of The University of Texas in Austin. Using her experiences as a registered nurse in the critical care setting, Overly applies the life lessons she learned from her patients and incorporates them into her literary works. Her emotionally driven novels evoke compassion as she gives a voice to difficult life issues that are often unspoken.

The Knot Series

The Knot Series Trilogy unfolds a romantic drama as evil trumps good, using the themes of art, tennis and ranching. The novels untangle struggles and interlock friendships as the main characters achieve emotional healing and self-confidence on their journey to find lasting love.

The Trinity Knot
The Zeppelin Bend (sequel to *The Trinity Knot*)
The Hitch (sequel to *The Zeppelin Bend*)

ACKNOWLEDGEMENTS

This book could not have been possible without the help of many people to whom I am forever grateful.

Thank you to my girlfriends who accepted the challenge as beta readers.

Thank you to the experts who shared their knowledge of life on a ranch and rodeo events and also knowledge about abortions and adoptions. You were so patient to answer all of my questions.

Thank you to my wonderful editors: Erin Liles and Emily Carmain for making *The Zeppelin Bend* a better book.

Thank you to my publishers, Marie and Mark, at Giro Di Mondo for their support in the continuation of my dream. I have learned so much from you.

Thank you to my husband for his understanding and help in making my dream a reality as well as his continuous love and support. Also, a special shout out of thanks to my son for saving my manuscripts, just in case.

Look for DonnaLee Overly's final book in the Knot Series
Coming in 2019

THE
HITCH

knots that bind

Turn the page for a sneak preview

CHAPTER 1

Gabby

Gabby watches her baby wave his small arms back and forth and her lips curve upward. She offers him her forefinger and he reaches for it and grasps on tightly. His strong grip surprises her. Looking down at his face, his eyes remind her of her daddy's. Already this little one has captured her heart with his bright eyes and sweet coos.

"I love you, my son." The kiss from her lips reveals the softness of his cheek and his gentle breath is intoxicating. She closes her eyes in amazement, and she marvels at the joy of motherhood.

"Gabby, Gabby..." A familiar voice calls but it is a faint echo. "I love you, Gabby. Please, don't leave me. You promised."

Yes, it is Brett's voice. She is excited to introduce him to little Jacob, the name they picked to honor Brett's father. Her smile widens as thoughts of their future dance in her head. They'll be happy. She is certain. A new trinity knot is created; it is her trinity knot that symbolizes family- Brett, Gabby, and Jacob. They are the three loops of the knot held together by their circle of love.

Suddenly aware that her arms are empty, Gabby yells, "Jacob, Jacob, where are you?" Her heart is racing and her breathing quickens. She struggles to move but her limbs are heavy and numb. Why can't she move? Why can't she open her eyes? Where is Jacob? All goes black.